Praise for HAUNTED:

'The author has an undeniable knack for *thrilling*, as few other writers have . . . he sure can tell a devil of a story'
The Literary Review

'James Herbert has the ability to write a novel which completely shatters any illusions you may previously have had about his writing, and HAUNTED is no exception'
Starburst

'Creepy and compelling'
Cosmopolitan

*Novels by James Herbert
Published by New English Library:*

The Rats
Lair
Domain
The Fog
The Survivor
Fluke
The Spear
The Dark
The Jonah
Shrine
Moon
The Magic Cottage
Sepulchre
Creed
Portent

HAUNTED

Haunted

James Herbert

NEW ENGLISH LIBRARY
Hodder and Stoughton

British Library Cataloguing in Publication Data
Herbert, James, *1943–*
Haunted.
I. Title
823'.914[F]

ISBN 0 450 49355 5

Printed and bound in Great Britain by
Mackays of Chatham PLC, Chatham, Kent

Hodder and Stoughton
A division of Hodder Headline PLC
338 Euston Road,
London NW1 3BH

*In memory of
George Goodings – rascal,
rogue, Dam Buster, and
my finest friend.*

To be haunted
is to glimpse a truth
that might best
be hidden

A DREAM, A MEMORY

A whispered name.

The boy stirs in his sleep. A pale, vaporous moon lights the room. Shadows are deep.

He twists his head, turning towards the window so that his face becomes a soft mask, unblemished, colourless. But the boy's dream is troubled; beneath their lids, his eyes dart to and fro.

The whispered name:

'David . . .'

Its sound is distant.

The boy frowns; yet the voice is within his own slumber, a silky calling inside his dream. His arm loosens from dampened bedclothes, his lips part in a silent murmur. His floating thoughts are being drawn unwillingly from their free-roaming hinterland towards consciousness. The protest trapped in his throat takes form, emerges as he wakens.

And he wonders if he has imagined his own cry as he stares through the glass at the insipid moon.

There is, in his heart, a dragging sorrow that seems to coagulate the blood, so that movement in his veins is slothful, wearisome, somehow making all effort to exist a ponderous,

11

perhaps even hopeless, affair. But the whispering, almost sibilant, voice dispels much of that inner lassitude.

'. . . *David* . . .' it calls again.

And he knows its source, and that knowledge causes him to shudder.

The boy sits up, rubs the moisture from around his eyes (for he has wept while sleeping). He gazes at the dim shape of the bedroom door and is afraid. Afraid . . . and fascinated.

He draws aside the covers and walks to the door, the trouser cuffs of his rumpled pyjamas caught beneath the heels of his bare feet, a boy of no more than nine years, small and dark-haired, pale-skinned and strangely worn for one so young.

He stands at the door as if fearing to touch. But he is puzzled. More – he is curious. He twists the handle, the metal's coldness leaping along his arm like iced energy released from a brumal host. The shock is mild against the damp chill of his own body. He pulls the door open and the darkness beyond is more dense; it seems to swell into the bedroom, a waxing shadow. An illusion, but the boy is too young to appreciate such natural deception. He shrinks away, reluctant to allow contact with this fresh darkness.

His vision adjusts, and the inkiness dissipates as if weakened by its own sudden growth. He advances again, timorously rather than cautiously, passing through the doorway to stand shivering on the landing overlooking the staircase. To descend this would be like sinking into the blackest of all pits, for darkness down there appears absolute.

Still the hushed whisper urges:

'. . . *David* . . .'

He cannot resist. For there is hope for him in that summons. A fragile hope, one that is beyond the tight and restricting bounds of sanity, but nonetheless the faintest denial of something so dreadful that he had become fevered with its burden.

He listens for a moment more, perhaps wishing that the peripheral voice would also rouse his sleeping parents. There is no sound from their room; grief has exhausted their bodies as well as their spirit. He stares into the umbra below, terribly afraid and, even more terribly, compelled to descend.

The fingers of one hand slide against the wall as he does so, their tips rippling over the textured paper. Disbelief mingles with the fascination and the fear, small lights – caught from who knows where? – glitter in his pupils, tiny twin beacons moving through the shadows, gleamings that slip jerkily into the depths.

At the foot of the stairs he pauses once again, glancing back over his shoulder as if seeking reassurance from his spent parents. There is still no sound from their bedroom. No sounds in the house at all. Not even the voice.

From ahead, at the end of the corridor in which he hesitates, comes a soft glow, a shimmering strip of amber. Slowly, each footstep measured, the boy goes to the light. He stops outside the closed door and now there *is* a sound, a quiet shifting, as though the house has sighed. It could be no more than a breeze stealing through.

His toes, peeking from beneath his pyjama legs, are bathed in the warm shine from under the door and he studies them, a delaying diversion from what he knows he must do next. The light is not constant; it flickers gently over the ridges of his toes. His hand grasps the doorhandle and this time there is no cold shock; this time the metal is wet. Or is it merely the wetness of his own palm?

He has to wipe his hand on the pyjama jacket before he can make the handle turn. Even so his grip is tenuous, skidding over the smooth surface before lodging and turning. A brief thought that there is someone clutching the other side, resisting his effort; then the handle catches and the door is open. He pushes inwards and his face is flushed by the lambent glow.

The room is a display of burning candles: their light bows with the opening of the door and their waxy smell welcomes him. Shadows momentarily shy away then rush forward in their own greeting as the myriad flames settle.

At the furthermost point of the room, resting on a lace-clothed table, is a coffin. A small coffin. A child's coffin.

The boy stares. He enters the room.

His step is leaden as he approaches the open casket, and his eyes are wide. The moisture on his skin glistens under the candlelight.

He does not *want* to look into that coffin. He does not *want* to see the figure lying there, not in such alien state. But there really is no choice. He is only a child and his mind is not closed to unnatural possibilities. Optimism may sometimes be bizarre in the very young, but it is no less potent for that. A voice has whispered his name and he has responded; he has his own reasons for grasping at the inconceivable.

He draws closer. The form inside the silk-lined casket is gradually revealed.

She wears a white communion gown, a pale blue sash tied at her waist. She is – she was – not much older than the boy. Her hands rest together on her chest as if in supplication. Dark hair frames her face and in her death she is almost serene, a sleeping, untroubled child; and although, in truth, she is perfectly still, unsteady light plays on the corners of her lips so that it seems she suppresses a smile.

But the boy, despite his yearning to disbelieve, knows there is no life within that pallid shell: the rituals of grief these past two days (not yet complete) were more convincing than her shocking absence. He is close above her, his brow pleated by a desperate longing. He wishes to speak her name, but his throat is constricted by the wretchedness of his emotion. He blinks, dislodging a swell of tears. He leans forward as if he might kiss his dead sister.

And her eyes snap open.

And she grins up at him, her young face no longer innocent.

And her hand stirs as if to reach for him.

The boy is frozen. His mouth is locked open, lips stretched taut and hard over bone, the scream begun but only breaking loose a moment or two later, a shrilling that cuts through the louring quietness of the house.

His cry wanes, dissolves, and the boy's eyes close as reason seeks sanctuary behind oblivion's velvet walls . . .

O N E

. . . His eyes opened and uncertainty surfaced with the wakefulness. The clatter of iron on iron, wheels on tracks, and the rhythmic lurching of the carriage banished the lingering shreds of his dream. He blinked once, twice, disturbed by gossamer after-images that had no clear form and certainly no context. David Ash drew in a breath and let his head loll to one side so that he could watch the passing scenery.

The fields were wearied by the season. Leaves, once crispy-brown now rain-soaked and dulled, were beginning to gather beneath the trees, leprous things discarded by their hosts. Here and there a house or cluster of buildings nestled against a hillside, a brief intrusion on the landscape with no prevalence at all over their surroundings. The late-autumn sky appeared as greyly substantial as the land it glowered over, a solid force whose lowest reaches softened hilltops.

Sudden blackness as the train entered a tunnel, the noise of its passage loudening to a hollow roar. A flaring of light, the man, alone in the compartment, revealed by the small flame.

Ash flicked off the lighter and the red glow of his cigarette cast deep shadows over his cheekbones and brow. He stared

15

into the darkness and tried to recall the dream that had left him so clammy-cold. It was as elusive as ever. He exhaled smoke, wondering why he was so sure it was the same dream that always left him feeling this way. Perhaps it was because of the faintest odour of candlewax remaining in the air – no, in his *mind* – afterwards; perhaps it was because it always took a while for his heartbeat to settle. Or perhaps it was *because* he could never remember this particular dream.

Daylight burst into the compartment once more as the train rushed through a deserted station. One day, Ash considered, glad of the distraction, there might be hardly any stopping-points at all between cities, towns and villages, the rail network becoming a vast arterial system with few minor organs to service. What then would become of these ghost stations? Would spectral commuters continue to line the decaying platforms, would the guard's warning to *Mind the doors!* still echo softly in the ether? Repeated images absorbed by concrete and board to be filtered back into the atmosphere long after the reality had ceased to exist. It was one of the Institute's standard theories regarding 'apparitions' and one that he endorsed. Would that prove to be the case in this new investigation? Perhaps not; but there were plenty of other explanations of so-called 'phenomena' to choose from. He watched cigarette smoke rise lazily in the air.

The train *clacked* over a level crossing, a solitary car waiting behind the barrier like some small animal mesmerized into immobility by a passing predator.

Ash glanced at his wristwatch. Can't be far to go, he assured himself. At least the journey had been restful, he'd had a chance to sleep . . . No, not so restful after all. The dream – whatever its content – had left him a little shaky. And his head ached dully, as it always did after the dream he could not remember. He touched fingertips to the inner corners of his eyes and squeezed gently to ease the ache. The pressure did not work, but he knew what would, an infallible cure. There was no buffet carriage on this train though, nowhere to get a stiff drink. Maybe just as well – it created a poor impression to meet a new client breathing alcohol with your first hello.

He rested his head against the seat back and closed his eyes, the cigarette dangling loosely from his lips, ash floating down onto his rumpled jacket.

The train sped onwards, hurrying through the countryside, occasionally slowing to a stop at favoured stations, few passengers alighting, even fewer climbing aboard. Towns and villages broke the landscape here and there, but mostly hills and pastures beneath a sullen and swollen sky, drifted by the compartment's windows.

The journey was over for Ash when the train pulled into the modest country station of Ravenmoor. He quickly hitched up his tie and shrugged on the overcoat that had been sprawled on the seat opposite. Pulling down a black suitcase and a holdall from the overhead rack, he rested them on the floor. He held the door ajar as the train came to a lumbering, squealing halt.

Stepping down, he reached back for his luggage, then slammed the door shut with an elbow. He stood on the platform, the only passenger to leave the train. The station appeared empty of all other life and the absurd notion that it was already a ghost station occurred to him. Ash shook his head, abashed that he, of all people, should entertain such a thought. A uniformed figure emerged from a doorway further along the platform and threw up a hand in an informal gesture towards the engine. The train began to pull away and the guard disappeared again without seeing his charge safely on its way. Ash waited for the last carriage to pass by before walking along to the station's single-storey building, the comforting clatter of wheels on tracks soon receding into the distance. The end of the train was just disappearing around a bend as he entered the gloomy ticket hall.

There was no sign of the guard inside and no one waiting to collect his ticket. An elderly couple were standing before the plastic window of the ticket desk, the man bending down to talk through the narrow money slot, ignoring the face-level grille. Ash strolled on through to the road outside.

No parked vehicles, no one coming forward to greet him. He frowned and placed the luggage on the kerb; he checked his watch. Ash stayed there for a while, studying what he assumed was the village high street. In immediate view there were a few shops, the inevitable building society, a Post Office – and The Ravenmoor Inn directly across the road. Hands thrust into his overcoat pockets, a fresh cigarette keeping him company, he waited for a car to pull alongside. That did not happen, so he paced the pavement, disliking the chill, a thirst itching at his throat.

A further ten minutes went by before he shrugged, returned to his case and holdall, and crossed the unbusy road.

The door of the inn opened on to a vestibule, with separate entrances to the bars on either side. Ash went through to the saloon and its occupants awarded him only brief attention. It was lunch-time active, but Ash had no problem in finding space at the bar, and no trouble in catching the barman's eye. The broad-faced man detached himself from a conversation and strolled over to the new customer with all the casual authority of a landlord.

'Sir?' he enquired, indifference to a non-regular plain in his expression.

'Vodka,' Ash ordered quietly.

'Something with it?'

'Ice.'

The landlord gave him a long look before turning to the optics. He placed the glass in front of Ash and dropped in two ice cubes from an ice bucket nearby. 'That'll be –'

'And a pint of Best.'

As the other man sidled away to draw bitter from a pump, Ash put two pound coins on the bar, then swallowed half the vodka. He leaned against the counter and let his gaze wander around the room. The inn was untypical of the usual 'Railway Tavern', for its low-beamed ceiling, large inglenook fireplace with polished horse brasses displayed over the mantel, declared more rural traditions. A thin man wearing a flat cap, his face blue-red with veins broken by harsh winds, watched him from a corner seat, eyes unblinking and cold. Three business types, hunched over snacks on a minute round table, burst into laughter at a hushed joke. A couple by the door, both approaching middle-age, sat close enough together for their thighs to touch and listened over-attentively to whatever the other was saying in the manner of a man and woman each married to a different partner. By the fire was a group in tweeds and mufflers, the men mostly satisfied to listen to the conversation of their womenfolk while they sipped their gin and tonics and pondered the virtues (or perhaps the boredom) of retirement. Generally, the buzz of chatter, a thin haze of cigarette and pipe smoke, the yeasty smell of beer from the cask. Reassuring and cosy if you were a regular, clannish and faintly inimical if you were an outsider.

He turned back to the landlord as his pint was settled on to a counter mat.

'D'you have a phone?' Ash asked.

The other man nodded towards the door. 'Through there. Where you came in.'

Ash thanked him and collected his change. He took his luggage over to a table beneath a window, then returned for his drinks, sipping the top of the bitter before carrying it and the vodka over to his seat. Discarding his overcoat, he made for the door, taking what was left of the vodka with him.

The payphone was further along the vestibule and he went to it, digging in his pocket for coins and laying them out on a narrow shelf next to the instrument. Sifting through with a finger he found a 10p and balanced it in the appropriate slot. He dialled a number and pushed in the coin when a girl's voice answered.

'Jenny, it's David Ash. Put me through to McCarrick, will you?'

A hundred or so miles away the telephone rang in an office of the Psychical Research Institute. Bookshelves filled with volumes on the paranormal and parapsychological, together with folders containing case histories of certain types of phenomena, lined the walls; grey, chest-high filing cabinets occupied the few gaps between shelves. A desk, its top cluttered with documents, journals and more reference books, faced a door that was ajar; a smaller desk, likewise untidy, took up space near a corner. A room crammed with the written word, but at that moment, empty of life.

The phone shrilled persistently and there were hurried footsteps outside in the corridor. The door was pushed wider and a woman, somewhat matronly in appearance, bustled in. She wore an outdoor coat and there were bright spots of colour on her cheeks from both the cold and the climb to the Institute's first floor. In her arms was a large bag and a bulging manuscript envelope. She hastily picked up the phone.

'Kate McCarrick's office,' she said breathlessly.

'Kate?'

'Miss McCarrick isn't here right now, I'm afraid.'

'Will she be long?' asked Ash, frustrated.

'David, is that you? It's Edith Phipps here.'

'Hello, Edith. Don't tell me you're into office work now.'

She gave a small laugh. 'No, I've just arrived. I'm having lunch with Kate. Where are you calling from?'

'Don't ask. Look, d'you think you can find her for me?'

'I expect s–' Edith looked up as someone entered the room. 'Kate's here, David. I'll just pass you over.'

She held out the receiver to Kate McCarrick, who smiled in greeting then raised her eyebrows questioningly.

'It's David Ash,' the older woman told her. 'He sounds grumpy.'

'When doesn't he?' Kate replied, taking the phone and moving around the desk to her seat. 'Hello, David?'

'So where's my reception committee?'

'What? Where are you?'

'Where the hell d'you think? I'm at Ravenmoor. You told me someone would meet me at the station.'

'They were supposed to. Wait a minute, let me get their letter.'

20

Kate left her desk and went to a filing cabinet. She slid open a middle drawer and riffled through the protruding name cards, her search stopping at MARIELL. She took the file back to her desk and opened it out: there were just two letters inside.

Ash's irritated voice came through the receiver. 'Kate? Will you –'

She lifted the phone. 'I've got it right here . . . Yes, a Miss Tessa Webb confirms she'll meet you at Ravenmoor Station. You caught the 11.15 from Paddington, right?'

'Yeah, I got it,' came the reply. 'And there were no delays. So where's the lady?'

'Are you calling from the station?'

There was a pause at the other end. 'Uh, no. There's a pub across the way.'

Kate's tone deepened. 'David . . .'

At the Ravenmoor Inn, Ash drained the remains of the vodka and swirled the ice around the empty glass. 'It's lunchtime, for Christ's sake,' he said into the phone.

'Some people eat for lunch.'

'Not me, not on an empty stomach. So what do I do now?'

'Call the house,' Kate told him, still frowning. 'Have you got the number on you?'

'You never gave it to me.'

She quickly scanned the correspondence before her. 'No, sorry. Miss Webb didn't include it in either of her letters. We've spoken on the phone, but it was she who rang me. Stupid of me not to have got the number then. You'll find it in the book though, under Mariell, the family name. I gather from her letters Miss Webb is a relative, or maybe just a secretary. The house is called Edbrook.'

'Yeah, I've got the address somewhere. I'll ring.'

Kate's voice was soft: 'David . . .'

Ash hesitated before hanging up.

'After you've called the house,' Kate said, 'why don't you wait for our client in the station?'

He sighed wearily. 'Presenting the wrong image for the

Institute, am I? Okay, this is my first and last drink for today. We'll talk later, okay?'

In the office, Edith noted the concern subduing her employer's smile.

'All right, David,' Kate said. 'Good luck with the hunt.'

Ash's farewell was flat: 'Have a nice day.'

Kate was thoughtful when she replaced the receiver and Edith, by now settled in a chair on the opposite side of the desk, leaned forward anxiously. 'Problem?' she asked.

Kate looked up, her attractive face breaking into a warmer smile. 'No, he'll be fine. Our client didn't turn up to meet him, that's all. Probably a confusion over time, or else she's running late.' She shuffled papers on her desk, retrieving an appointments book which had been buried. 'Two sittings for you this afternoon, Edith,' she said on finding the appropriate day. 'A widow, freshly-made, and an elderly couple who want their son's death confirmed. Would you believe he was reported missing as long ago as the Falklands conflict?'

Edith shook her head regretfully. 'The poor dears – so many years of uncertainty. They want me to locate his spirit?'

Kate nodded. 'I'll give you details over lunch.' She pushed back her chair and stood. 'Personally, I could eat a horse. But I'm counting on you to stop me.'

'Perhaps we could share it.'

'You're not much help, Edith.'

The psychic smiled up at her. 'We'll just have to remind each other of the calorie count when we eat. Not that you couldn't do with a few more pounds. Now, tell me more about our widowed friend while we walk . . .'

Ash thumbed through the local directory he'd found inside a shelf beneath the telephone. He muttered as he scanned the Ms. Where the hell was Mariell? He turned the page, looking for variations in spelling. Double-R? No such name. He flicked to the back section, looking for Webb. A few of those hereabouts, but no T for Tessa. And none of these Webbs lived at a place called Edbrook. On a chance, he tried the Es. No, not listed under Edbrook, either. He cursed under his breath; Miss Webb should have told Kate that the Mariells were ex-directory.

He was about to slam the book shut when a hand lightly touched his shoulder. Ash shivered as cold air breezed through the open doorway.

T W O

She was small and dark-haired, her skin pale and her features delicate. Her smile was apprehensive.

'David Ash?' she asked.

He nodded, for a moment, ridiculously, unable to speak. A glint of amusement was in her eyes now.

'You're Miss Webb, right?' he said at last.

'Wrong,' the girl replied. 'I'm Christina Mariell. Miss Webb is my aunt. I persuaded her to let me fetch you from the station.' Her head inclined to one side as she studied him. Then: 'Sorry I missed you.'

He cleared his throat, realized his whole body had tensed. Ash smiled back at her. 'That's okay,' he said. 'I needed some nourishment anyway.'

Her attire was simple: a long coat, slim-fitting, curving in gently at the waist, hardly swelling at all over her breasts; the shoulder padding was squarish but by no means exaggerated, the collar tight around her neck. He couldn't decide if she were ultra-stylish or hopelessly old-fashioned; not that he had any real sense of such things.

'I wanted to be the first to meet you,' she told him as though excusing her presence.

Ash was surprised. 'Oh yeah?'

'It's exciting. I mean, a ghost hunter . . .'

'No, it isn't really. How did you know who I was?'

The girl held up a copy of a book and his own monochrome image frowned back at him. 'You're a *someone*,' she said.

Ash grinned. 'True. It sold at least three hundred copies. Can I buy you a drink?'

'My brothers are waiting for you back at the house. We really should go.'

Ash hid his disappointment. 'If you're sure . . . let me get my luggage from the bar.'

She turned to him, saying, 'I'll wait for you outside.'

He stared after her, a little bemused. Then he shrugged and returned to the saloon bar to drain half the pint of bitter before picking up his case and holdall. He nodded towards the thin man with the veined face, who continued to watch him from beneath the flat cap with no apparent interest, then went through to the vestibule once more, this time stepping out of the main door into the autumnal day.

He stopped to appreciate the car in which Christina Mariell sat waiting. It was a model he hadn't seen in many a year, and only then in magazine features on popular old cars. The Wolseley's bodywork and wheels appeared to be in immaculate condition and its engine was running smoothly with only a mild escape of exhaust fumes from the rear. The girl leaned across and pushed open the passenger door, her smile the invitation.

Ash shoved the suitcase over onto the backseat and eased himself into the front, keeping the holdall on his lap. 'Some car,' he commented. 'There can't be many still around of this era.'

She gave no reply but engaged first gear and pulled out into what little traffic there was. When they were some distance along the high street, she said: 'What do you drive?'

'Uh, nothing at the moment. Another four months before they let me back on the road again.'

She looked at him and he caught the surprised amusement.

'You don't imagine I'd use British Rail by choice, do you?'

Christina returned her gaze to the road, the smile still playing on her lips.

'So tell me,' Ash said.

She was puzzled, but the smile remained. 'Tell you what?'

'Why your family is so keen to have me on this job.'

She kept her eyes on the way ahead. 'You've got quite a reputation for solving mysteries of the paranormal.'

'The irregular normal, I prefer to call it.' He shifted the bag on his lap so that he could stretch his legs. 'There are other investigators employed by the Institute just as good as me.'

'I'm sure there are some almost as good, but it seems that you're the best. My brother, Robert, made extensive enquiries before deciding on you. And you came highly recommended by Mrs McCarrick. We've also read your articles on the para–' she gave a small laugh '– sorry, the "irregular" normal, as well as your book, of course.'

'Who's we?' he asked, interested.

'Both my brothers, Robert and Simon. Even Nanny's shown an interest.'

'Nanny?'

'Nanny Tess. My aunt . . .'

'Miss Webb?'

Christina nodded. 'Nanny's looked after us all since my parents died. Or perhaps we've taken care of her, I'm not sure which.'

There were fewer houses on either side as the car reached the outskirts of the village. The stubby tower of a church rose above gravestones like a flint conduit to the heavens; someone in black looked up from their insular mourning as the car sped by, pallid face as bleak as the monuments around.

'And all of you have been made aware of this . . . haunting?' Ash asked, returning his attention to the girl. 'I believe that's how Miss Webb referred to it in her letters to the Institute. You've all experienced the phenomena?'

'Oh yes. Simon first saw –'

He held up a hand. 'Not just yet. Don't tell me about it now. Let me see what I can find out for myself to begin with.'

'You won't know what to look for.'

He saw that her hair was auburn, its shade depending on the light she was in. And her eyes were blue, tinged with grey. 'I don't need to at this stage,' he explained. 'If you really are being haunted, then I'll know soon enough, won't I?'

She was smiling again. 'Not even a hint?'

And he returned the smile. 'Not a whisper. Not yet.'

The two pills felt ridiculously burdensome on Edith's tongue, like swollen pellets, difficult to dislodge. She took a gulp of Perrier water, washing away the sour debris in one swallow. There, you devils, she said in her mind, enough of your arrogance; now go about your business and keep this tired old blood flowing.

She thanked the waiter with a smile as he placed fillets of sole before her, then looked across the table at Kate who was glumly surveying an egg and anchovy salad. Edith shook her head. 'I should be the one punishing myself with health food,' she said with only the faintest hint of guilt.

'This is the price I'm paying for a weekend's indulgence,' Kate replied, squeezing lemon over lettuce. 'However, penance is one thing, masochism is another.' She reached for her white wine and took a long sip. She shrugged at Edith. 'It compensates.'

The psychic saluted her companion with the Perrier as though it were champagne. She noticed the faintest of lines around Kate's eyes, a certain tightness around the mouth, first hints that 'prime' was beginning its metamorphosis into 'maturity'. Still, forty was no longer regarded as 'over the hill' for a woman and Kate certainly had the kind of handsome looks that would follow her into old age. Unlike me, Edith considered, who never had had the sort of features she'd wished to follow her into later years. No, for some people the ageing process was a bonus (count me among them, she

27

thought) whereby 'awkwardness of countenance' mellowed and became absorbed into the whole. Perhaps that was why the really old looked so alike, a unification in physical balance, almost a return to the uniformity of birth.

'Edith, you're miles away,' Kate's voice interrupted.

The psychic blinked. 'I'm sorry. My mind wanders too much these days.'

'Not unusual for a medium.'

'Our thoughts need direction.'

'Not all the time. This is lunch, remember? You can relax.'

'Like you?' Edith gently chided. 'When was the last time you completely relaxed, Kate?'

The other woman looked genuinely puzzled. 'I have no problem with that at all – you should see me at home.'

'I wonder. The Institute is always so busy, and with the Parapsychological Conference imminent . . .'

'Well, yes, the annual conference always presents a lot of work for us, especially when we're the host country.'

'And the many investigations you're involved in?'

'Most so-called paranormal phenomena take no more than a few hours for our investigators to dismiss as perfectly natural happenings, even though the circumstances might be unusual.'

'But others can mean weeks, even months of painstaking study.'

'True enough. Let's be honest though, they're the ones we like.' Kate sliced egg and began to eat. 'Incidentally, I think the case that David is on might prove interesting – it could be a genuine haunting. I just hope he handles it correctly.'

Edith, picking up her knife and fork, leaned forward. 'Are you worried about him?' she asked.

Kate smiled distractedly. 'Not as much as I used to be.'

'Now what does that imply? Does it mean you're no longer so involved with him, or that he's a little more settled?'

'I hadn't realized it was common knowledge that we'd become "involved".'

'Why should it be a secret? You're divorced, he's unmarried, you see a lot of each other – a reasonable assumption for people to make, wouldn't you agree?'

Kate shook her head. 'Our relationship was never that serious. An occasional "thing" I suppose you could have called it.'

'Less occasional now, though.'

'A good deal less.'

Edith tasted her fish and refrained from adding salt. 'He's an unusual man,' she said after a while. 'I'm surprised you've lost interest.'

'I didn't say I had.'

'Then he –'

'David can sometimes be too absorbed in his own cynicism to allow much room for a developing relationship.'

'Or too absorbed in his work,' Edith suggested.

'It more or less amounts to the same thing.'

The older woman pondered her companion's response. 'I see what you mean . . . He has such an active prejudice against all things spiritual, I often wonder why he and I are friends.'

Smiling, Kate reached over and touched the medium's arm. 'It's nothing personal, Edith. He regards your type of sensitive as misguided, but sincere. I think he appreciates the comfort you give to the bereaved. No, it's the outrageous charlatans that he despises, the kind who practise deceptions for their own profit. You're different, and he's aware of that; he really believes you can help people.'

'And how does that sit with you, Kate? Having two such opposing factions under the same roof.'

'The Institute's research has to have balance. We need people with honest scepticism such as David's to give credibility to our genuine findings on paranormal occurrences.'

'Even though he attacks much of that evidence, genuine or not?' Edith lowered her voice as a couple were shown to a table nearby. The restaurant was busy, a hubbub of conversations and movement. 'Many of my kind hate him for his

29

constant negative reaction against us. They look upon him as a threat to their own validity.'

Kate was insistent. 'But many others – outsiders – regard that attitude as positive. Let's face it, Edith: David has an impressive record for exposing phonies and for explaining hauntings or certain psychic phenomena in perfectly rational, materialistic terms.'

'You sound as if you're on the side of the sceptics.'

'You've known me for too long to think that. But as a director of the Institute I have to keep *my* mind open to the logical as well as the illogical, don't you see?'

'Of course I do,' Edith replied. There was a sparkle in her eyes when she added, 'And I know how often you accept the logical when every instinct tells you otherwise.'

Kate laughed and acknowledged her friend's point with a raised glass. She sipped the wine, then resumed her half-hearted attack on the salad lunch.

Edith's expression was serious when she ventured, 'But David's conflict is far greater than yours.' She laid down her fork and drank more of the Perrier while Kate watched her.

'I don't understand,' the younger woman said.

'You don't? Surely you've suspected? Goodness, you know him too well not to.'

Kate's tone was mild. 'Edith, what exactly are you getting at? Are you telling me David has some dark secret he's kept hidden from me all this time? Something locked in his closet, like his manhood, for instance? I can assure you, you couldn't be more wrong . . .'

Edith held up a hand, smiling as she did so. 'I accept your word for that, Kate dear. No, I mean something far more important. Have you never realized that David has the gift? Or perhaps it should be called the curse.' She gave a brief shake of her head. 'Oh, his psychic ability is repressed, severely so, but it's undeniably there. His problem is that he won't admit it, not even to himself. And I don't know why that should be.'

'You've got to be wrong,' Kate protested. 'Everything he

does, says . . .' She waved a hand in exasperation. 'He's dedicated his life to disputing such things.'

Edith gave a small laugh. 'If you'll excuse the expression, Kate, it takes one to know one. My thoughts have met David's more than once, but he's always managed to lock me out very quickly. It's like automatic shutdown with him.' She toyed with her food, her attention elsewhere. 'Can you imagine the turmoil going on inside his poor mind? As you say, he's spent years disproving something that subconsciously he knows to be true.'

'I can't accept that, Edith. David is far too level-headed for that kind of neurosis.'

The psychic looked directly into Kate's eyes. 'Level-headed? Is he really, Kate? Are you honestly that sure of him?'

Kate did not reply to the question; but her uncertainty was evident.

THREE

The Wolseley sped through country lanes, the girl by Ash's side an assured driver (although he would have preferred her to ease up on the speed). The woods bordering the roads were thick, the dwellings sparse. They passed a telephone box at a junction, several panes of glass missing, grass grown high around its base. A rook pecked at a small furry carcass lying by the roadside; the bird hopped back onto the verge as the car passed, something stringy dangling from its beak. Only here and there were there glimpses of fields and hills beyond the trees, such holes in the forest's fabric quickly passed by.

Ash glanced at the girl occasionally, liking the gentleness of her features, the eyes that held a barely-suppressed humour, almost a mischievousness. Christina hummed a tune, something childlike in its simple cadence, and each change of gear was light, despite the vehicle's age, her hand shifting the lever with delicate grace as if it offered no resistance at all.

The dullness of the day was unremitting, the clouds like one vast lumpy sheet, smudged darker in parts, ragged edges few.

There was no further conversation between Christina and Ash, although once or twice she turned his way to give him a smile, her attention immediately going back to the road, allowing him no time to respond.

Soon the car pulled into a driveway, the large, ornate gates at the entrance open wide, a long gravelled lane in some need of repair stretching ahead. The gardens on each side, after a brief expanse of woodland, were mainly laid to lawn, but the nearer the Wolseley drew to the house itself, the more elaborately landscaped they became. The flower beds, the trimmed hedges and shrubbery, had obviously been designed to present a variety of views, each one depending on how it was approached. The house reared from the gardens as though its architect had intended it to dominate rather than blend with the surrounds: Edbrook was imposing in its greyness and, despite swelling apses and well-ruled bay windows, somewhat disconcerting in its bleakness. Inexplicably, something seemed to lurch within Ash, an abrupt sagging of mood that left him strangely wearied. He peered up at the house and wondered at his own unease.

Christina brought the car to a halt below a short flight of stone steps that led up to Edbrook's entrance. She switched off the engine and jumped out, taking the steps with energetic skips as the front door began to open.

Ash alighted at a more considered pace, reaching back into the Wolseley for his luggage and standing in the drive for a few moments to take in his surroundings.

A woman was in the doorway above, her face anxious as she watched the investigator.

'I was late, Nanny,' he heard Christina say, 'but I soon found our Mr Ash.'

He climbed the steps as the woman addressed as Nanny opened one half of the double door wide, daylight revealing her grey hair and lined face. She stepped back to allow Christina through and Ash nodded to her as he followed.

'Miss Webb,' he said.

There was a nervousness in her scrutiny of him, almost as if she were suspicious as to his true identity. 'Thank you for coming, Mr Ash,' she said at last, evidently satisfied.

It took a while for his eyes to adjust to the gloom of the cavernous hallway he found himself in, daylight having little force against the shadows within, while oak panels covering much of the walls added their own sombreness. Directly opposite was a broad staircase rising to a galleried landing, the hallway itself narrowing towards the back of the house, doors leading off on either side.

Two men were waiting by the foot of the stairs.

The elder of the two – in his mid-or-late-thirties, Ash guessed, and soberly dressed in suit and tie – strode forward, a hand extended.

'Permit me to introduce myself,' he said, his welcome as formal as his attire. 'I'm Robert Mariell, and this is my brother, Simon.'

The younger man came towards Ash with less reserve than his brother, although there was little effort in the handshake. His white open-necked shirt and V-collared sweater over loose-fitting trousers, together with his short hair-style, gave him an air of jovial boyishness, this abetted by his spoken greeting of 'Marvellous.'

A stirring in the shadows behind the two men drew Ash's attention. A sliver of darkness that must have been a partially opened doorway beneath the staircase was broadening, a shape slipping through. There was a low, menacing growl before the dog came into view.

Ash could not help but tense. The dog was unlike any breed he knew, its bulky shoulders standing over two feet from the ground, coat black and wiry, though shaggy in length, its head rectangular and skull flat, muzzle powerful. The animal skulked forward, eyes that were almost oval fixed on the stranger.

'And this is Seeker,' Robert Mariell said, stooping to pat the dog's flank. Its head rose high from its shoulders, and its steady gaze never left the intruder. 'Don't let him alarm you, Mr Ash. It takes him a little time to get used to strangers.'

Perhaps not alarmed, but certainly uncomfortable, Ash replied: 'So long as he's been fed recently . . .'

Simon Mariell laughed delightedly. 'We won't let him bother you. Come on, Seeker, back to the cellar where you belong.' He ushered the dog to the open doorway and it obediently went through.

On noticing Ash's puzzled expression, the older brother said, 'A *Bouvier des Flandres*, Mr Ash. A Belgian cattle dog, in fact, and rather special, don't you think? They can be very ferocious when roused and they really are as powerful as they look. Rather good, actually, for keeping away unwelcome visitors.'

Ash relaxed only when the cellar door was closed.

'Now, may we offer you some lunch?' Robert Mariell asked. 'You must be hungry after the journey down.'

Ash declined. 'Uh, no. I had something in the village.'

'I hope my sister didn't keep you waiting too long.'

The investigator returned Christina's smile, then looked around the hallway and at the gallery above. 'What I'd really like to do is unpack, then inspect the house and grounds.'

Simon rejoined the group, hands in his trouser pockets. 'But why the grounds? We usually come across our ghostly visitor inside.'

'There may be outside causes for what's happening in here,' Ash answered.

'Underground springs, subsidence, forgotten tunnels . . . ' Robert suggested.

'You've done your own research.'

'All from your book on the subject. Nevertheless, I don't think you'll find anything like that in our garden.'

'Do you have a detailed map of the estate?'

Simon interjected. 'Oh, Christ, you won't need anything like that. The problem really is inside. Look, we ought to tell you what each of us has seen . . .'

Christina spoke up. 'No, Simon, Mr Ash doesn't work that way. He likes to find out these things for himself.'

Ash looked from one to the other. Nanny Tess – Miss Webb – remained by the open door as if she might be expecting him to leave at any moment. 'Well,' he said, 'let's say I like to sense a mood first, then look for any faults in the structure of the building, the land around . . .' He walked over to one of the walls and rapped his knuckles against the panelling. 'Rotten timbers and secret draughts can be responsible for a hell of a lot of so-called manifestations. At some stage I'll want to talk to each of you individually, find out what you've personally experienced.'

Nanny Tess finally left her position by the door, although still she did not close it. Her voice was anxious. 'How long will this take, Mr Ash? Will you be here for very long?'

A little taken aback by the earnestness of the question, he replied, 'That depends. The whole investigation could take no more than a day, or it might take a week. Let's see if I strike lucky.'

'You're our guest for as long as you wish,' Robert assured him smoothly. 'We're all rather keen to get to the bottom of these, er, these disturbances. Perhaps we can discuss them over dinner this evening, after you've completed your initial survey?'

'That's fine by me.'

Nanny Tess sounded almost regretful when she said, 'I'll show you to your room then.'

Ash picked up his luggage, acutely aware that his hosts were watching him closely. He followed the Mariells' aunt to the stairs, but paused when Robert spoke.

'There is just one point I'd like to make before your investigations begin.'

Ash raised his eyebrows in question.

'Nothing you discover,' the other man went on, 'must go beyond the walls of this house and the records of the Psychical Institute. We're a very private family and the locals hereabouts would like nothing better than to have stories of "ghosties" and poltergeists up at Edbrook to giggle over. And God knows what the county rag would make of it.'

Ash nodded in agreement. 'I may have to visit the nearest town's council offices or library to look into the history of this place, but don't worry, I'll be discreet. All anyone will have to know is that I'm doing a structural survey of the property. And whatever I *do* find here – whether it can be explained or not – will be a private matter between yourselves and the Institute. Unless you change your mind and want the whole thing publicized, of course.'

He began climbing the stairs, but Robert's voice brought him to a halt once again.

'Then you do believe certain things are inexplicable. I was under the impression that you held no belief in the supernatural as such.'

'Inexplicable doesn't necessarily mean supernatural,' the investigator answered somewhat resignedly. 'It only shows we don't have the knowledge to understand. Not so far, anyway.'

Robert regarded him with a blank expression, but as Ash turned away to resume his journey, he caught the secretive smile that passed between Christina and Simon.

FOUR

Nanny Tess walked ahead of him along the dim corridor, her small shoulders slightly hunched, her footsteps unusually loud on the wood flooring. There was a dampness to the air, and a smell of dust, as though windows in the house had remained closed for a long time. Curtains at the far end of the corridor were only partially drawn so that light scarcely penetrated.

The woman in front paused to tell him that the bathroom was further down on the right before opening a door on her left. She allowed him to go through, then stood in the doorway as he dropped his luggage onto the bed. 'I'm sorry I wasn't there to meet you at the station . . .' she began to say.

He shook his head, tired of apologies. 'That's okay – really.'

'Christina can be very wilful.' Regret seemed to taint her smile. 'She hid my car keys so that I couldn't come and fetch you myself.'

Ash was surprised. 'She was that keen to meet me?'

The tone was almost wistful, as though Nanny Tess were thinking of other times. 'She enjoys her little games. They all enjoy their games.' She suddenly straightened, dismissing the reverie, her manner abruptly brisk. 'If you need anything, just let me know – my living quarters are on the floor above this one. We have dinner at seven, so you'll have plenty of time to look over the house.'

'And the gardens,' he added.

'Yes, the gardens too.' She left the room, quietly closing the door behind her.

Ash scanned the room, relieved that at least it was brightened (albeit dismally at that moment) by light from a south-facing window. The bed was large, with sturdy head and end boards; he tested its softness with a hand and was satisfied that it was more comfortable than it appeared. A bulky oak wardrobe stood against the wall facing the bed, and a high chest of drawers was by the door. Bedside table with lamp, huge rug covering most of the floor, a small writing bureau, this too with lamp. It'll do, he told himself; for a couple of days, at any rate. Ash saw no reason for the investigation to take longer, even though he had warned the Mariells it might. For some obscure reason, he hoped it wouldn't.

He opened up the suitcase after throwing his overcoat onto the bed, and began to unpack equipment he would use in the investigation: Magnetic tape recorder, two cameras, one a Polaroid, both with flash and capacitance detectors, extendable tripods, thermometers, magnifying glass, measuring tape, graphite powder and flour, strain gauge/spring balance, as well as other items that might prove helpful such as graphite paper, compass, voltmeter.

He placed the smaller pieces inside the drawers of the chest and the cameras on top, tripods by the side. A micro-tape recorder he put in his jacket pocket, a small notebook in the other side. Ash rolled up the heavy cloths that had separated and protected the contents and closed the suitcase, snapping the lock shut. Stretching, he hoisted the case on top of the wardrobe, then returned to the bed and unzipped the holdall. He removed underwear and a change of clothing, transferring them to the wardrobe and the drawers not already occupied, then took out toiletries, laying them on the bed for the moment. The last item lying at the bottom of the bag was a vodka bottle. As he reached for it the faint sound of laughter came in through the closed window.

Breaking the cap's seal, he went over to look out at the grounds below. He took one swallow of vodka only, then replaced the cap. Ash frowned when he saw someone skulking through the shrubbery outside.

It was Simon Mariell and he was grinning as he crouched among the bushes. Ash caught sight of another figure approaching. She was dressed in white and, although she had her back to him, he recognized Christina's auburn-coloured hair, the curls where it touched her shoulders. He heard her call Simon's name as she searched. She laughed aloud and her brother sank lower in the bushes, a hand over his mouth to suppress his own mirth.

Ash edged closer to the window, bemused by the childish game being played below.

Something else moved, not far from the other two figures. Someone by a tree, watching the players too. A younger girl . . .

Simon was creeping from his hiding place and for a moment Ash was distracted. When he looked back towards the tree, the third figure had disappeared.

His attention went back to Christina and, foolishly, he almost called out to warn her that Simon was now stalking her. He stopped himself, his knuckles already poised at the glass. He smiled, amused that he had almost been caught up in their game.

Yet the girl was beginning to turn towards him as if she had sensed she was being observed.

He held his breath without knowing he was doing so.

Her head was tilting upwards towards the window, the motion slow and, feeling embarrassed, Ash wanted to step back out of sight. But he was held there in a kind of fascinated paralysis, wanting their eyes to meet.

Her profile was swinging into view so slowly that he realized his mind had strangely accelerated his own thoughts, creating the illusion of languor in her movement. It gave him time to wonder whose unguarded moment had been invaded – hers or his own? Who was the voyeur – Christina or himself?

Her face was almost in view, one shoulder pointing at him – when there was a sharp knock on the bedroom door.

He blinked, startled. In reaction, he turned from the window.

The door opened. Christina peered in.

'Are you ready to see around the house now?' she asked, smiling brightly.

Ash was too surprised to answer. He looked back through the window.

The other girl had gone. The garden was empty.

FIVE

There was a coldness about Edbrook which only in part was to do with the shift in season. In certain rooms and corridors there was a dankness of air, in others a sense of emptiness that suggested they had not been used – nor, perhaps, even entered – for some years. It was a large house though, and of a type Ash had investigated more than once before: it was not unusual for such homes (mainly due to inheritance taxes if the property was passed down through the family) to be frugally managed. It was not as though Edbrook had been neglected so much as that its upkeep appeared to be economically directed.

Christina guided him through the upstairs rooms, including those in the attic, then downstairs through the library and drawing room, sitting room, kitchen, scullery, dining room and study. He tested floorboards and panellings, fireplaces and chimney breasts, sometimes rapping against the walls, often just listening for natural sounds, occasionally standing still to feel draughts and determine from where they came. He hesitated at the top of the cellar steps, remembering the *Bouvier* had been ushered down there. But Christina, already descending, laughed and chided him for his faint-heartedness. She assured him that Seeker would not harm him unless it sensed he was a threat, and that was extremely unlikely, wasn't it? Ash followed her, albeit cautiously. The dog grumbled from somewhere in the shadows, but did not show itself.

The cellar contained rows of half-filled wine racks, a fine coating of dust matting the bottles. Oddments littered the area – pieces of furniture, some covered by dustcloths, broken statues, empty picture frames – and on one side there were gloomy alcoves with shapes inside that Ash could not discern. The chill here was acute, which rendered the basement a fine wine cellar; more important to him, though, it indicated that there might be subterranean springs close by or fissures in the immediate strata causing freezing draughts to seep in through the aged and cracked brickwork. An interesting location in terms of the investigation but, mainly because of the unfriendliness of the Mariells' dog, not one in which he wished to linger for too long.

Ash and the girl climbed the stone steps and he was uncomfortably aware that Seeker had wandered from its resting place to follow.

It was with a mild sense of relief that Ash left the cellar to walk through the kitchen and scullery out onto the garden terrace. Although he found it difficult to be caught up in Christina's overt enthusiasm for the house and its grounds, he could easily imagine that at one time Edbrook had provided a grand home for the Mariell family; what was lacking now was difficult to define, but it had something to do with ambience, a distinct lack of warmth (and not necessarily of the physical kind). A fine place for a haunting, he surmised. *If* one believed in such things.

He looked out over the gardens, disappointed that on close inspection they were not quite as tidy as at first appeared. Nevertheless they were magnificently laid out in formal yet interesting lines and curves, the dense bordering woodland providing a perfect backdrop. He breathed in deeply, as if to rid his lungs of stale air collected inside the house.

'How long have you been searching for ghosts, Mr Ash?'

Christina asked with a hint of mischievousness in her smile.

He answered her seriously. 'I don't search for ghosts: I look for causes of unusual disturbances. And my name's David – I'd rather you called me that.'

'All right, David – how long have you been seeking out mysterious causes?'

He grinned at her. 'Man and boy, it seems. The phenomena always interested me to some extent, but it was only when I went to my first seance that I really got hooked.'

'How old were you then?'

'Oh . . . early twenties.' He shook his head reflectively. 'I was a trainee engineer at that time, believe it or not. God knows what prompted me to attend a seance – curiosity, I guess, and a natural progression of my interest. You see, although I could never understand people's belief in such things, I couldn't help wanting to know more. That first seance really opened my eyes.'

Christina came to a stop. 'You actually made contact with the spirit world?'

Ash laughed. 'Just the opposite,' he told her. 'I was almost fooled for a little while – the medium was that good. He had us all convinced we were seeing the ghost of one of the sitters' long-lost relatives, a dear-departed granny who began to tell the woman next to me all the illnesses she had suffered over the last ten years. The woman's illnesses, that is, not the granny's – *she'd* never been so healthy since she'd arrived on the other side.'

Ash shook his head again, amused by the memory. He continued to walk across the broad, stone-flagged terrace, Christina keeping pace with him, glancing up at his face from time to time.

'The whole scene was bizarre,' he went on. 'I could see a kind of misty form hovering in the gloom behind the medium, and I must admit there was a cold, creepy feeling running up my spine. But it was the trivia granny was coming out with through the medium that set me giggling.' He chuckled at the thought. 'I expected something profound, maybe something deeply moving, an insight into this spiritual world on the other side of our own life, if you like.'

'And . . .?' she prompted when Ash fell into a thoughtful silence.

'Uh, all we heard was that Uncle Albert's false teeth were lost somewhere in the drains beneath his house – he'd flushed them down the toilet after an evening's heavy drinking, along with most of what he'd drunk. Yet the woman next to me looked as though she'd just learned the whereabouts of the Holy Grail. I glanced around at all those faces, and oh God, they were so *serious*. That started me laughing like a hyena.'

Although still smiling, his tone was grim. 'I don't know, it was somehow a huge relief to me, a weight lifted off my shoulders. Because the whole business was farcical. My attitude didn't go down too well with the medium, of course. He ordered me out, and I was pleased to go. But before I went through the door, I flicked on the light switch – call it malice, or maybe it was genuine curiosity.'

They passed the French doors to the drawing room of the house, the room empty as far as Ash could tell. Edbrook rose above them, louring in its greyness, sullen in its silence. He consciously moved away from the edifice, uneasy in its shadow.

'With the light, everyone in the room was able to see that "granny" was no more than an old photograph back-projected onto fine muslin. Just to help the effect, steam was coming from a tube in the wall and swirling through the material to move the image. Pretty impressive in the semi-darkness, but not so hot in the light.'

Christina's eyebrows had arched. 'But the things she told the woman . . .'

'Useless information that could easily be gained from a friend or relative of the client – probably whoever introduced her to the circle in the first place. You see, the medium only had to find out about one or two of the sitters to amaze everyone else around the table.'

'They must have been furious when they saw how it was done.'

'Yeah, they were. Mostly with me.'

'You?' she said in disbelief.

He nodded. 'I'd shattered their hopes. They weren't going to thank me for that.'

Christina and Ash walked on in silence for a while. There was incredulity in the girl's voice when she spoke again. 'Surely they're not all fakes? There must be some genuine mediums.'

'There are,' he replied. 'I know several. One or two are even friends of mine. But I can't explain what they do and how they do it. I'm only certain that they don't talk with the dead.' They descended a short flight of steps, the stone path before them branching off in three directions around the flowerbeds. They continued along the centre path. 'It's only when we begin to understand what's going on inside our own minds that we'll discover some answers to the paranormal.'

Christina frowned at that: 'What happened after? You must have been disillusioned yourself.'

'Not disillusioned. Like I said – it was a huge relief to have my doubts confirmed. Yet I was even more intrigued. Was it all a sham? Everything I'd read about the paranormal, everything I'd heard? I delved further, researched a lot, and before I realized it, the whole business of finding out had become a career. And the more deceptions or mistakes I unearthed, the more angry I became.' A low wall spread out from the centre of the formal garden, its stonework scarred and crumbling. 'Then a few years ago, the Psychical Research Institute invited me to work with them. I guess they'd rather I was spitting out than in.'

Christina's assertion was unexpected. 'You believe we're being foolish about the haunting of this house. That makes you angry, too.'

'Not at all. I just think you're mistaken. It shouldn't take long to find out.'

They had reached the knee-high wall and now Ash could

see that it encompassed a large ornamental pond, almost a miniature lake, the water stagnant, a murky brown, full of weeds and rotting waterlilies. The sight came as a shock, for although the gardens themselves were not as carefully kept as they might have been, the degenerated state of the pond was surprising.

Ash stared into it, and its sour stench caused him to catch his breath.

He turned to the girl but, unnoticed, she had stopped some distance away. She looked past him at the unwholesome pond almost as if it had come as a shock to her also, that she hadn't realized they had walked this far. There was something skittish in her movement as she backed away.

'Christina . . .?' he said wonderingly.

Behind him, the turbid water rippled, reeds and tendrils stirred . . .

. . . There was a light sheen of perspiration on Edith's brow. She jolted in the chair and her eyes sprang open, the image in her mind instantly gone.

The elderly couple sitting opposite regarded her with concern. 'Mrs Phipps?' the white-haired man said, leaning forward anxiously. 'Are you all right? You were telling us of our son . . .'

Edith blinked and it was moments before she realized she was in one of the Institute's private rooms. The precognition had broken through her contact with this couple's son, a young seaman who had perished during Britain's last war in circumstances too cruel to relate to his still-grieving parents.

'I'm . . . I'm so sorry,' she told them. 'I lost my concentration. I'll . . .' she drew in a breath to steady herself '. . . I'll try to reach Michael again.'

But when she closed her eyes the image returned, although it was unclear.

She was looking up at the figure of a man, someone who

had his back turned towards her. Even so, she knew it was David Ash. As well as the odd angle, there was something else wrong with the vision, for it had wavered before her as if . . . as if she were watching him through water . . . dirty, muddy water. There were moving fronds around her, reeds shifting like loose tentacles. Two naked arms reached up for David, slender, pearl-white limbs, fingers clawed. Yet they were not *her* arms, not Edith's. They belonged to another.

And even though they stretched through the disturbed water towards the man above, rotted plants curling around their wrists, these arms were bloodless.

They were dead things.

S I X

The dining room was feebly lit, candles on the long table around which the Mariell family and David Ash sat casting a warm but barely adequate glow, some of the wall lights behind the diners not functioning at all. Ash had half expected a maid or at least a housekeeper to be in attendance, but Nanny Tess herself had served the meal without even assistance from Christina. By now it was apparent to him that the Mariells were not quite as wealthy as they obviously had been in the past. Nevertheless, although he was curious about the family, the financial aspect of their lives had nothing to do with the job in hand. He sipped wine wishing it were something stronger.

Christina giggled at something Simon had whispered to her and, at the head of the dining table, Robert Mariell rebuked them both with a stern glance. His sister raised her fingers to her mouth and cast her eyes downwards, suitably abashed, while next to her, Simon continued to smirk.

Robert directed his attention towards Ash, who sat facing him at the opposite end of the table. 'How did your investigations go today? Did you locate any secret draughts or leaks that could explain our little mystery?'

Ash cut into the roast beef before him, the meat somewhat

49

overdone for his liking. 'That's impossible to say,' he answered, 'since I don't yet know what your little mystery is. But I found plenty of structural faults in this place that could possibly create disturbances of some kind.'

Still grinning, Simon asked: 'Serious enough to create a ghostly figure, Mr Ash?'

'You'd be surprised how what may seem like ghostly forms can be caused by dust or smoke. Or how dripping water, channelled through a hidden conduit, can be transformed into ghostly tapping. Regular contraction of floorboards, for instance, starting from the nearest source of heat such as a fireplace or radiator, each board releasing pressure on the one next to it, can sound like spectral footsteps. With some help from our own imaginations, anything's possible.'

Nanny Tess, seated on his left, and who had hardly touched her food, interrupted. 'The visions I've – we've – seen are not just creations of our minds. If you knew –'

Ash raised a hand. 'Tomorrow. Each of you can tell me what you've experienced tomorrow. I want to remain totally objective for now, no preconceived notions.'

'But I still don't see how you can know what to look for,' Christina protested.

'I'm looking for some kind of phenomenon and I gather it takes the shape of a ghost. That's all I need to know for the moment.'

The merest smile touched Robert's lips. 'Do you believe in such things, Mr Ash? Lost spirits, things that go bump in the night . . .?'

'. . . Banshees,' said Simon excitedly, 'demons, vampires . . .?'

'. . . Werewolves?' Christina joined in.

Simon howled like a wolf, and she laughed aloud. Even Robert smiled broadly.

Unamused, Ash looked at Nanny Tess, who avoided his eyes. She, too, did not appear to find their antics humorous.

He addressed himself to the older brother. 'For a family experiencing haunting, you don't seem unduly alarmed.'

'Should we be?' came the reply. 'Can such manifestations physically harm us?'

Ash shook his head. 'Not usually. Any harm is generally caused by the witnesses to themselves when they panic.'

'Then why should we be concerned? But you still haven't answered my question: Do you, yourself, believe in ghosts?'

'It depends on how you define such things. Apparitions, telepathic visions, electro-magnetic images. You might even call them vibrations of the atmosphere. They can exist without our comprehending their meaning or exactly what they are.'

'But you wouldn't describe them as spirits of the dead?' asked Nanny Tess.

All eyes were intent on the investigator. He cleared his throat, and stared back at them in turn. 'No, not at all,' he said. 'Not in any of my investigations has the existence of life after death ever been proved conclusively to me. And I've exposed too many so-called spiritualists as frauds to give conversations with the dead much credence.'

'So we understand, Mr Ash,' said Robert mildly. 'But you don't believe we're lying to you?'

'Of course not. Whatever it is you've experienced here at Edbrook is obviously very real to you. Why else would you pay for my services? I'm only saying that what's happened may have some perfectly rational explanation.'

Simon rested his elbow on the table, chin on his hand. 'I think you really should be told –'

'All in good time,' Ash repeated. 'Let me find out what I can for myself first.'

'You may not necessarily experience what we have,' Robert commented.

'I shouldn't imagine for a moment that I would. The psychic link may only exist between you four and whatever's taking place. We'll see.'

'Psychic link?' Simon sat upright again. 'What, exactly, is that?'

'Imagine, if you can, that our minds are like some kind of radio receiver. You, as the occupants of this house, may be tuned in to somebody else's transmission.'

Simon considered the suggestion as amusing. 'Somebody's broadcast from the other side . . . ?' He looked around at his family, apparently seeking approval for his mockery.

Ash did not rise to the bait. 'Let's call it a thought process from someone now in another place, or an impression they've left behind. It might be that you, because of your association with Edbrook, are tuned in to that particular wavelength.'

'A very interesting proposition,' admitted Robert. 'But not really acceptable, is it?'

'No less than the idea of ghosts,' Ash replied.

Christina dabbed her lips with a napkin, the glow from the candles soft in her eyes. 'And what can we do to help you with your investigations – apart from tell you what we've seen for ourselves?'

'Not much, except stay out of the way,' he told her. 'Later this evening I want to set up some equipment around the house, mainly at certain points I think might be susceptible to odd occurrences. Once that's done I'd like you to keep away from those areas. In fact, it would help considerably if you kept to your rooms for the rest of the evening.'

At this last request the Mariells and their aunt glanced around at each other.

'That's a bit drastic,' protested Simon.

'Only for tonight,' Ash assured him. 'Maybe afterwards we can concentrate on one or two specific areas.'

'You'll have our fullest co-operation,' Robert answered for them all. 'Is there anything else you need?'

'Not for the moment. Oh, I'd like to ring Kate McCarrick a bit later, just to let her know how things are going.'

'Nanny Tess tells me Miss McCarrick was enthusiastic about our choice of you for this investigation. She appears to think highly of your work.'

'She's something of an authority on the subject of parapsychology herself. I must admit, we don't always agree in our views, but then the whole field is more conjecture than proven fact. Incidentally, if my tests at Edbrook prove positive it might be an idea if she came here with an impartial observer.'

The sharpness of Nanny Tess' response startled him. 'No, no,' she insisted, 'that won't do at all.'

Robert's rejection of the investigator's suggestion was more relaxed. 'As I've already stressed, Mr Ash, we want to keep this affair very low key. I think you can appreciate our reasons.'

'There'd be no publicity involved,' Ash promised. 'It'd just be a matter for the Institute, for the records.'

'Let's take your investigation one step at a time, shall we?' the older Mariell said evenly. 'That was your own wish, wasn't it?'

Ash smiled wryly. 'Okay. No pressure whatsoever from me. It's all in your hands.'

Robert eyed him coolly from the far end of the table. 'Not entirely. No, I wouldn't say that at all . . .'

He jiggled the telephone contacts frustratedly, holding the bulky black receiver close to his ear with the other hand. Not a thing. The line was dead. As stolidly reliable as the machine presented itself, it was useless. Did these old pieces eventually wear themselves out, or was the fault somewhere in the system beyond these walls? Whatever, it was a bloody nuisance.

He wheeled around on hearing a footstep in the hallway behind him, at once surprised by his own nervousness.

'Miss Webb,' he said, surprised even more by his relief. 'Uh, the phone – looks like you've been cut off.'

She was close to him, peering up into his face. 'We're always having trouble with the lines,' she said. 'That's one of the few disadvantages of living in the country.' She took the receiver from him and, without bothering to check it for herself, rested it on its cradle. 'I'll do something about it when I go into the village tomorrow.'

Her eyes were intent on him and he wondered if the anxiety in them was merely her usual expression. She was a small woman, almost frail in build, and he guessed she was somewhere in her late sixties or early seventies. What was she to Christina and her brothers? An aunt, yes, but what else? As far as he could tell, she ran the house for them, and that had to be quite a task for someone of her age.

'Mr Ash . . .' she said, then hesitated to say more.

He waited.

It was almost a whisper. 'You will take care while you're here at Edbrook, won't you?'

He could not help but grin. 'I told you: Spooks can't touch us. They shouldn't even frighten us really, not when we know their true cause.'

'There are different ways to be . . .' again the hesitation '. . . haunted.'

'I thought you understood my views –'

Her retort was sharp. 'No, you're the one who doesn't understand.'

'Then explain it to me,' he said stiffly.

But another voice interrupted before she could answer. 'Our investigator doesn't want his head filled with your silly notions, Nanny.'

They looked up to see Robert Mariell watching them from the stairs.

'Isn't that right, Mr Ash?' His expression was only mildly reproving.

Ash turned back to the aunt. 'I'll be asking questions tomorrow,' he told her patiently, puzzled by her behaviour.

'Then we'll leave you in peace,' said Robert. 'Come along, Nanny, let our guest get on with his work. Good night to you, Mr Ash. You won't be disturbed again.'

With that he turned and disappeared into the darkness at the top of the stairs. Avoiding Ash's gaze, Nanny Tess hurried after her nephew.

Ash watched her diminutive figure climb the stairs, then shook his head. It seemed that the Mariells' aunt was not as keen on Edbrook's 'ghost' as the rest of the family appeared to be.

SEVEN

Ash spent the rest of the evening setting up equipment around the house. Four thermometers, whose lowest reading during the night would be registered, were placed against walls or rested on furniture; tape recorders with noise-actuation devices were located in the library and kitchen; cameras linked to capacitance change detectors, so that any movement in the vicinity would trigger off shutters, were set up in the drawing room and study; at certain points, both upstairs and down, he sprinkled a fine layer of powder on the floor, and across one or two doorways he stretched black cotton.

Later, by lamplight, he sat in his room and studied rough plans he had drawn up of Edbrook, with its labyrinth of rooms and corridors, occasionally taking a nip from the vodka bottle standing within hand's reach on the bureau. He smoked one cigarette after another as he made notes in a pad and now and again he would glance towards the window where the night seemed to press against the glass.

Eventually he left the room to roam the house, treading warily around powder patches, not entering those places containing detection instruments, nor disturbing doors with cotton stretched across.

Edbrook was quiet. And it was still.

Somewhere in the house a clock chimed the late hour. Ash, using a flashlight for guidance, walked the length of the corridor, passing his own room, heading for the window at the far end. Even though he was tired physically, his senses were acutely alert, as if his mind were a restless passenger inside a rundown vehicle. Kate McCarrick's considered diagnosis of his usual condition was always clear-cut: 'You drink too much, and smoke too much. And one day – it may be some time in coming, David, but it'll happen – your brain will be dulled as your body often is.' Might be no bad thing, Kate, he thought. No bad thing at all.

He reached the window and switched off the flashlight, standing close to the glass to see beyond. The blanket clouds had finally given way, although not entirely: milky-edged cumuli remained, almost motionless, tumbled in the night sky like frozen avalanches. The moon had a space all of its own, as though its white-silver had eaten away the surrounding clutter, and deep shadows were cast across the lawns and gardens below the window. There were forms down there other than those arboreal, statues whose clearly-defined shadows pointed towards Edbrook like accusing fingers. From a distant place amidst the wooded areas came the hollow shriek of a night creature, a sound no less disturbing for its faintness.

Ash looked on, but his gaze did not rove, for his thoughts were directed inwards at that moment. The piteous, animal cry had stirred a memory, one more distant in his own mind than its catalyst from the trees. He remembered the sharp, human screech that had once skited across rushing water and possibly the vision would have emerged as a whole had not a noise from behind caused him to turn.

He flicked on the flashlight and shone it along the corridor, the beam swift to repel the blackness. The light caught a vague movement by the stairway.

Without hesitation, Ash hurried towards it and as he approached he realized that the fine powder he had laid earlier that evening was swirling in the air as though caught by a wind.

57

He stopped at the edge of the billowing, torchlight catching a million tiny motes in its glare, and stared in astonishment. There was no breeze that could flurry the dust so, and no person who might have caused the disturbance was on the stairs. He quickly checked a thermometer hanging nearby from a light-fitting on the wall and was alarmed to find the temperature was close to zero. Yet he felt no chill himself.

More sounds. From below. Like bare feet on wood.

Ash went to the balcony and peered over, shining the light into the hallway there. He glimpsed something grey or white disappearing round a corner.

Quietly, no more than a loud whisper, he called: 'Christina?'

He moved to the stairs, brushing the still-swirling powder away from his face as he passed through. Descending hastily, he swung the beam around the hall until satisfied that all doors were closed, his attention then caught by further sounds. He pointed the light down the hallway towards the rear of the house, certain that the noises had come from the kitchen area.

As he went off in that direction he noticed the door beneath the stairs – the cellar door – was slightly ajar. He stopped, aware that he had shut it earlier, but another sound from ahead sped him onwards.

Ash entered the darkened kitchen, the flashlight darting from table to cupboards, sink to old iron ovens and grate, dresser to window. The low snarling seemed terribly close.

He turned too quickly, the torch catching the doorframe, the light instantly snuffed. With less control than he would have liked, Ash scrabbled on the wall by the door for the lightswitch, his fumbling fingers finding and striking down. The light was dull, but enough for him to see that the kitchen was empty. And that a door opposite, which he knew led to the terrace and gardens, was open.

He heard someone outside, a muffled giggle.

Leaving the broken flashlight on the table, Ash went through the kitchen and out into the night.

Bright though the moon was, it was several moments

before his eyes adjusted to the contrast, and a second or two longer before he could be sure of what he was seeing. A figure dressed in flowing white was flitting across the terrace. It suddenly vanished from view.

Ash's eyes narrowed, his face washed in moonlight. Again, almost under his breath, the question: 'Christina?'

He followed, breaking into a slow run, reaching the steps that led down from the terrace into the gardens. He searched for the figure in white, certain that he had lost sight of it at this point. Yet nothing moved among the flowers and shrubbery below.

Ash descended and took the centre path towards the pond, eyes seeking left and right. He reached the low crumbling wall and looked down on the water, its still surface shiny with moonlight, the silver sheen somehow compelling.

His fascination was broken by the sound he had heard before – the soft padding of footsteps. Only this time they were hurried, and the bare feet were against flagstones.

He whirled around to face whatever it was rushing towards him, but was struck by a powerful force so that he hurtled backwards, the wall catching his legs, sending him toppling.

Stagnant water closed over his head, its grip cold and slimy. Ash struggled in panic as weed tendrils clutched him. He twisted frantically, their grip tightening. Clouds of mud stirred and swelled sluggishly so that the moonlight ceiling above was smeared.

As he fought to free his arm of syrupy fronds he saw, sinking towards him through those eddying clouds, a silhouette, a shape whose arms were outstretched, as if crucified, whose flimsy robe billowed and swayed with the currents, whose black hair spread outwards in Gorgonian tresses.

Foul-tasting water gushed in to stifle Ash's scream.

. . . Edith woke, her eyes springing open, the nightmare still vivid.

She pushed herself upright in the bed, trembling and terribly afraid. But afraid not for herself.

She whispered his name . . .

'David . . .'

Her breathing was laboured, its sound harsh in the moonlit bedroom. She forced calmness upon herself, steadying her breaths with concentrated effort. Her hand gently soothed the skin over her heart.

Edith sank back against the headboard, the heaving of her chest gradually subsiding. She stared at emptiness. But she saw those white and dead hands once more.

Hands that were clutching at David Ash.

E I G H T

Ash twisted in the water, perhaps to turn away from the silhouetted spectre floating towards him, perhaps to break free of the clinging weeds. Perhaps neither. He was drowning and the overwhelming awareness of that alone left little room for other terrors.

Yet through this horror of imminent death he felt an arm encircle his throat from behind.

Bubbles spewed furiously from his open mouth as he was dragged backwards. Ash struggled but his efforts were feeble, for already a mist was dulling his thoughts, a sluggishness leadening his limbs. For one brief and peculiarly lucid moment he was in another time – an instant of *déjà vu* – fighting weakly against tumbled water, a rough hand pulling at him, lifting him . . .

And he was clear, cold night air rushing at him as overwhelmingly as had the stagnant water he was now emerging from. Other hands clutched at his clothes, cruelly pinching the flesh beneath. He was rising, being hauled over the wall that encircled the moonlit pond that was no longer placid but heaving with the swell created by his own struggles. Someone was pushing him upwards from below and, as he rose, Ash glimpsed Simon's face, wetness slicking the younger man's

61

hair flat against his forehead. Something hard scraped against his back and then he was lying on the uneven flagstones, vomiting the liquid contents of his stomach and lungs.

He floundered there on the puddled stone, shoulders racked and limbs twitching, choking and then gasping air alternately, his head light with dizziness.

Ash had no idea how long he remained so, but when he finally collapsed onto his back, chest still rising and falling spasmodically, there were faces peering down at him. Simon, Robert, and Nanny Tess, their nightclothes soaked, the younger of the Mariell brothers completely bedraggled.

Ash tried to speak, tried to tell them, one shaking hand pointing back at the pond. But his words were almost incoherent.

'Someone . . . someone else . . . in there . . . Someone was holding me . . .'

Robert Mariell leaned forward, touching Ash's shoulder reassuringly. 'You're all right now. Just take it easy and get your breath back.'

Ash managed to get an elbow beneath him. 'No! There's . . . there's someone else . . . a girl . . . in the water . . .'

Robert exchanged curious looks with his brother and aunt. Ash was convulsed by a coughing fit as he tried to push himself further upright. He wiped away water from his eyes and mouth.

'Nanny, would you turn on the pond lights,' he heard Robert say.

Ash looked up at them again and Nanny Tess moved from view. Christina took her place, her face expressionless.

He rolled onto his side, coughing more water, his eyes closing tightly. He had thought . . . But no, Christina's nightclothes were not even wet. Nor was her face, her hair. A flaring of light caused him to open his eyes again.

Ash forced himself to stand, feeling someone helping him, but not knowing whom. He staggered the few feet to the low wall, his sodden clothes heavy, weighing him down, and sank to his knees to search the pond. He felt the presence of the others around him, but did not look up. They said nothing as they, too, watched the floodlit water.

There was no disturbance in those murky depths, merely a stirring of its surface.

He frantically scanned the weed-ridden water, even dipped in a hand to clear floating scum. Breathing was still painful, but he managed to say, 'I followed someone from the house. I heard someone running . . .'

'Ah, I think I understand,' he heard Robert say.

Ash turned towards him, then followed the direction in which Robert Mariell was looking, away from the pond, back towards the terrace. Something was lurking there, crouched low to the ground.

Robert snapped his fingers and the dog edged forward, almost sullenly. 'I'm afraid you were chasing Seeker. We allow him to roam the house at night.'

'No, no,' Ash protested. 'I saw a girl. She was running . . . running away from me.'

'That can't be so, Mr Ash. Unless you, Christina, were wandering around in the moonlight . . .?' Robert smiled at his sister, his question not meant to be taken seriously.

She shook her head, a small frown furrowing her brow. 'I was asleep in my room. All the noise woke me.'

Using the wall for support, Ash pushed himself up. He was still weak, still trembling, and he sat on the crumbling brickwork, resting his elbows on knees, face buried into his hands.

'No, there was –' he began to say, but Robert interrupted.

'I heard footsteps outside and went to my bedroom window. I saw only you out here, Mr Ash, no one else.'

'But in the water . . .'

'Seeker mistook you for an intruder. He attacked, you fell into the pond. Perhaps it was fortunate that you did – Seeker can be extremely ferocious.' He indicated the weeds still gently stirring in the dark water. 'You became entangled in . . . that mess. You panicked, you imagined someone holding you.'

Ash shook his head.

'There can be no other explanation,' Robert went on, undeterred. 'Unless, of course, you met our ghost . . .'

Ash's hands came away from his face and his eyes were wide as he stared in turn at each of the Mariells. He could not be sure, such was his shock and now confusion, but when his gaze met Christina's there seemed to be the faintest shadow of a smile on her lips.

Kate raised the brandy glass and her companion on the sofa moved closer. He clinked her glass with his own, then leaned forward to kiss her lips. She responded, but not seriously, soon parting to sip the brandy.

Harcourt smiled, then drank from his own glass. His dress tie hung loose around his fly-collar, the evening suit jacket unbuttoned, the beginnings of a paunch grateful for the freedom. Lamplight from behind reflected unflatteringly through his thinning, blond hair.

'I enjoyed this evening,' Kate said quietly, her fingers twisting the squat stem of the glass. She eased off her left shoe with the toe of the right, repeating the manoeuvre on the other with her stockinged foot. Her legs stretched out beneath the long gown and her shoulders sank back into the soft cushions of the sofa.

'There's more . . .' her companion intimated.

Her reply was playful. 'Too much of a good thing . . .'

'You deserve to be spoilt.' He leaned closer to her again. 'I'm in no mood to leave, not tonight.'

Kate raised her eyebrows. 'The cat's away, I take it.'

He shook his head. 'Uh-uh. This *rat's* away. I'm on business. Out of town as far as Helen's concerned.'

Kate frowned. 'I don't like these games, Colin.'

'I'm deadly serious, old thing.'

Despite the lightness of his tone, she saw that he was. 'It isn't what I want –'

The ringing of the phone from the hallway interrupted her.

Harcourt looked at his watch. 'Christ, it's a bit late for phone calls, isn't it? Leave it, let them go away and bother someone else.'

With a sigh, Kate struggled from the sofa. 'It might be important. It'd *better* be, this time of night . . .' she muttered, going through to the hallway.

Harcourt moodily sipped his drink as he listened to Kate's voice from the open doorway.

'McCarrick, hello?' A pause. 'Edith . . . is something wrong?'

In the sitting room of her small terraced house in the city suburbs, Edith Phipps clutched her nightgown tightly to her throat. She sat in a wicker chair by a table big enough only to hold a telephone and lamp. She looked around furtively, almost as if the night shadows might be eavesdropping.

Her voice was agitated when she spoke into the mouthpiece. 'Kate . . . listen to me. I think something has happened to David.'

'What are you saying, Edith?' Kate McCarrick's tone was as anxious. 'Have you heard from him?'

'No – I woke from a dream.'

There was a hint of exasperation in Kate's question. 'A dream? Edith, do you know what time it is?'

'I'm sorry, Kate, I didn't mean to disturb your sleep . . .'

'You didn't,' the voice at the other end said as Edith continued speaking.

'. . . but it was so vivid, so frightening. I saw David drowning.'

Kate was firm, her unease hidden. 'Calm down, now. It was only a dream.'

'No, it was much more than that,' Edith insisted. 'He's in danger, I sense he's in danger. Everything was so confused . . . David was under water, something was dragging him down. He was so afraid . . .'

'Are you registering a precognition?'

'Please don't go official on me, Kate. I'm calling as a

friend. There is something very wrong at this house David is investigating. I have this feeling of dread for him.'

Kate was aware that her own anxiety was growing, despite her irritation. 'If you're concerned, then so am I. Unfortunately there isn't much either of us can do tonight. Listen, I'll contact the Mariells first thing tomorrow.' She noticed Harcourt in the doorway leaning against the frame, drink in hand, watching her. 'He should have called me from there this afternoon, but perhaps he was too busy setting up equipment – I understand Edbrook is a large house.'

'Can't you call tonight?'

Kate forced herself to resist the medium's urgency. 'No, that would be ridiculous. It's far too late to disturb them.'

'Kate . . .'

She was adamant, but her voice softened. 'Please don't worry, Edith. You know, it really might have been just a bad dream. Don't you remember we were discussing David over lunch? Perhaps it triggered off something in your sleep.'

'If you won't, then let me phone the house now.'

'You know that isn't possible. The Institute's clients are guaranteed absolute discretion – I can't even discuss the case with you. And besides, I don't have the number, I'll have to go through Directory tomorrow.' Kate eyed the brandy in Harcourt's glass, feeling in need of a stiff shot herself. 'Now please go back to bed and try to stop worrying – this kind of thing won't do your condition any good at all. I promise I'll be in touch as soon as I have news, good or bad.'

'Please, Kate . . .'

'*Good night*, Edith.'

The medium blinked when the line was disconnected. She studied the receiver for several moments before replacing it. Edith stared at the opposite wall, her mind on David Ash.

Kate was thoughtful as she turned away from the phone. Her way was blocked by the tall figure of Harcourt. 'That sounded fraught,' he said.

'One of the Institute's resident spiritualists,' Kate replied distractedly. 'She was quite upset.'

'Obviously a neurotic type.' He grinned disdainfully.

'Normally she's as down-to-earth as you and I.'

'Down-to-earth? Someone who converses with ghosts? Come on, Kate, I accept you take your job of researching such things very seriously, but there must be times when even you find it difficult to swallow.'

'Not very often, as a matter of fact.' Kate brushed past him, going back into the lounge where she picked up her brandy. She turned to him as he followed her. 'I think you should leave now, Colin.'

Harcourt stopped dead. 'Hey, what did I say? I wasn't knocking you, nor the Institute. I know how dedicated you are. It's not always easy for us ordinary folk to understand what it's all about though.'

'I'm aware of that. But I'm a little tired.'

'Preoccupied, you mean,' he retorted.

'I don't want to argue. The evening's been too nice for that.'

'Well, let's continue it then. Look, I'm supposed to be away on business.'

'Tell your wife you got through quicker than you thought you would. It'll be a nice surprise for her.'

Harcourt was incredulous. 'You're serious?'

Kate nodded, going to the door.

'What the hell's got into you?' Harcourt stared at her, incredulity turning to exasperation. 'Is it something to do with this man you were talking about on the phone? This . . . David, wasn't it?'

'I'm just tired. Please go, Colin.'

Harcourt thumped down his brandy glass on a coffee table and strode to the door, collecting an overcoat draped over an armchair on the way. 'I'll never understand you, Kate,' he said with more resignation than bitterness.

Kate's reply was apologetic. 'I'll ring you tomorrow.'

He paused in the doorway. 'Maybe you shouldn't bother.'

'Maybe you're right.'

With a twitch of disgust, Harcourt disappeared into the

hallway. Kate blinked at the slamming of the front door.

She sank down onto the sofa, the brandy glass held over her knees. Her face was troubled, and her thoughts were of David Ash.

Perhaps she should have accompanied him on this case, as she had on other occasions in the past. She remembered the last time, more than a year ago . . .

N I N E

'When was the last time you went to church?' asked Kate.

'Now there's a question,' Ash said.

'Whatever, there's a chance for you to catch up on all you've missed.'

He took the vodka from her and pulled a face when he tasted the tonic she'd added.

'Neat poison will kill you.' Kate sat beside him on the sofa. She pushed at the heels of her shoes, working them off, then settled back against the cushions. She sipped her wine while Ash waited for her to explain.

'An interesting case turned up today, one I'd like you to handle,' Kate said at last.

'Does it mean taking the cloth?'

'No, but it'll mean spending some time inside a church.'

'A haunting?'

'More like a possession, from what I'm told.'

He rose from the couch, going to the cabinet where he added more vodka to his drink. Kate shook her head resignedly.

'So,' he said, returning, 'tell me more.'

'Two people came to my office this morning with a strange story, one that, I'll admit, I had difficulty in swallowing. The fact that they were clerics helped. And both seemed quite rational.'

'Priests coming to the Institute for help?'

'One was a vicar, a Rev Michael Clemens. The other was his rural dean. The vicar's parish is in Wrexton.'

'Where the hell is that?'

'Not far from Winchester. A small market town.'

'Should be pleasant enough.'

'Not according to our reverend. He's losing his flock, apparently. His parishioners are becoming frightened to set foot inside his church. It seems they believe demons have taken charge of the place.'

Ash grinned, unable to help himself.

'Come on, David. The poor man's sincere. More than a bit troubled, to be honest, but as I said, quite rational.'

'Shouldn't he and his rural dean be consulting with their superiors rather than us?'

'Oh, they have. Rev Clemens first took it to this rural dean, who then, after matters got worse, referred it to their bishop. It was the bishop who gave them the go-ahead to contact the Institute, but only on the understanding that the whole thing would be handled discreetly.'

'Naturally.'

'Naturally. Something like this could make the Church look pretty silly. I got the impression that the rural dean was dead set against the whole thing. He was under instructions though, so had no choice but to agree to a cold, scientific and, importantly, an impartial investigation.'

'This vicar must have been convincing.'

'Why do you say that?'

'In my experience, the Church – of whatever denomination – likes to take such matters under its own wing. If they have devils to be cast out, they have the know-how. Why bring in outsiders and leave themselves open to ridicule?'

'Because this so-called "possession" has become common knowledge in the town. Some of the townsfolk are enjoying the fun of it all, while others are quite frightened. The bishop wants it stopped before too much harm is done, and he feels an organization of repute such as our own can do just that.'

'I suppose it makes sense. When do I start?'

'We. I'm joining you on this one.'

Ash was surprised. 'Any special reason?'

She looked away from him. 'It'll give us a chance to spend a little more time together. We both seem so busy nowadays . . . Besides, it's been a while since I've been out in the field, as it were. I need to get involved more directly sometimes.'

He wondered if there was yet another reason. Was Kate coming along to keep an eye on him? Was adding tonic to his vodka a gentle hint, a way of saying I'm on to you David, I've heard the whispers, even received one or two complaints, and now I'm watching you? He knew also that it wasn't just the Institute's reputation Kate cared about: she was concerned for him. And he found that more irritating than touching. Drink wasn't a problem; it was easily handled. No, the disquiet within was the troublemaker, his very own demon; and it was this that was difficult to deal with, for it had no focus. Because of that, because he could not comprehend its source, its pervasiveness was not easy to resist. Alcohol, at least, dulled its effect.

Kate reached for his hand and he consciously stopped himself from drawing away. 'I thought we could drive down to Wrexton tomorrow,' she said. 'Will you stay here tonight?' The question was casually put, but her thumb momentarily ceased stroking his knuckles while she waited for the reply.

'I'll need some things.'

'We could collect them from your place on the way.'

He wondered why he was searching for other reasons not to stay. What the hell was wrong with him?

'Your enthusiasm is overwhelming,' Kate said.

'I'd really love to stay tonight. This is me begging.'

Too late, of course, but her hand tightened over his.

'Perhaps we can talk later,' she said.

She meant when they were naked together, bodies touching, darkness isolating them from all else but each other. A time of vulnerability and responsiveness.

'Do we need to?' he asked, the weight of his question obvious to her.

She closed her eyes briefly. 'You know we do.'

They *had* needed to, but they didn't talk later that night. Kate made the attempt, but even she was exhausted by their lovemaking. David might be moody, might be annoyingly introverted at times but, she mused, he never lacked passion. And thank heaven for that.

Kate steered the Saab off the roundabout, heading for Winchester. There should be a sign for Wrexton soon. She took a look at Ash and saw that he had dozed off, his head sagging forward, chin almost touching his chest. Thanks a bunch, she thought. Always nice to have good company on a long drive. At least he'd offered to use his own car, but one, she didn't like its condition, and two, she didn't like the condition in which he sometimes drove. He wasn't totally irresponsible, but one day they'd get him when he was just over the limit. Might be a good thing if they did.

David, wake up, she said silently, wake up to yourself. For both of us, before it's too late.

'Wake up, David,' she said aloud. 'We'll soon be there.'

He did.

But, she thought, not to himself. Not yet.

The church door was half-open. Ash stepped through and received no comfort: if anything, it was cooler inside the building than out. Were churches always this cold? Spiritual warmth was one thing, but attendances might be up if these places of worship also provided physical warmth. He went to the centre aisle, the echoes of his footsteps sharp and loud. He amused himself with the notion of ghostly pacing, a step behind his own.

Ash paused, looking down the wide aisle towards the nave and altar. Nothing sinister here, he told himself. Just miserable gloom. For Ash, there was nothing uplifting about the high altar with its cross and candlesticks, its linen cloth drably grey in the dismal light from the stained glass windows. He was about to turn away when he noticed someone kneeling at the communion rail.

He heard voices behind him, one of them belonging to Kate, and he glanced over his shoulder to see her and, he assumed, the Rev Michael Clemens entering by the door that he, himself, had used moments before. Rev Clemens was in his early- or mid-forties and was thin of face and frame, perhaps his strongest feature the glasses he wore, horn-rimmed, the lenses thick around their edges. When Kate introduced the two men to each other, the vicar's handshake was a single jerked gesture; he offered no smile, only anxiety.

'Thank you so much for coming,' he said. 'Perhaps you will be able to convince my bishop that St Mark's is no longer the place for Christians.'

'I think you've got the wrong idea,' Ash replied. 'My intention is to prove that there *isn't* anything unholy going on here. At least, not in the sense of a genuine haunting.'

The cleric looked at Kate. 'But I thought –'

'In most cases of so-called paranormal or supernatural activity investigated by the Psychical Research Institute the cause is usually found to be perfectly natural, although the circumstances may be mysterious,' she told him. 'David has a certain expertise in unravelling those mysteries.'

'I see.' Rev Clemens seemed disappointed. 'I think you might not be so successful on this occasion.'

Ash was moderate in his reply. 'I should tell you that this kind of thing is nearly always the work of vandals or the mischievous. If not, it's likely to be someone with a personal grudge against the Church or even against you, yourself.'

'I assume you've been told what has happened here.'

Kate answered. 'David likes to begin his investigations with as little prior knowledge of whatever the occurrences might be as possible.'

'No preconceived ideas, you see,' Ash explained. 'But maybe this case could be an exception.'

Kate eyed him in surprise.

'It might save us a lot of time,' he said directly to her.

'Blood, Mr Ash.'

Both returned their attention to the Rev Clemens.

'Blood smeared on walls and statues. Holy vestments soaked with it. I arrived one morning to find the christening font filled with blood.'

'Excrement anywhere?'

'I beg your pardon?'

'People who break into churches with malicious intent like to defile them in the foulest ways possible. Excrement and urine are the easiest and most obvious means.'

'No, nothing like that. Nothing as disgusting.'

'Blood is pretty disgusting. Where are these vestments? We could get the blood analysed.'

'I'm afraid I burnt them. I had no wish to be reminded of such sacrilege.'

'Pity. What other violations?'

'Two nights ago the dossal – that's the curtain at the back of the altar – was set alight. It was fortunate that the whole church didn't go up in flames.'

The vicar led them up the centre aisle towards the nave, pointing at statues spaced along the side aisles as they went. 'See how they've been broken, marked. I, myself, scrubbed them clean of the more obscene and diabolic disfigurations.'

Ash was curious when he saw that the kneeling figure at the communion rail had gone. A stout pillar blocked his view, but he assumed there was another door just beyond. As they drew nearer to the altar he realized his assumption had been correct, for there was a deep yet narrow recess in the wall. A small side-door was just inside.

'The church organ has been battered beyond repair,' the vicar was saying. He pointed up at the pulpit. 'The carvings have been chipped, there are scratches in the wood that resemble claw marks. Look at this side door.' He took them over to the recess Ash had already noticed. 'It seems to have been attacked with an axe. It's the same back there with the entrance door.'

'I hadn't noticed,' said Ash.

'Why should you? These marks are on the *inside*. They weren't made by someone trying to gain entry, Mr Ash.'

Ash frowned as he studied the smaller door.

'And then there are the candles. More than once I've found every candle in the church alight or burned down when I've arrived for morning devotions.'

'The vicarage is close by,' said Kate. 'Haven't you heard or seen anything suspicious?'

'Miss McCarrick, I've kept vigil through the night on several occasions, and nothing around St Mark's has stirred. The only sound I've ever heard coming from here in the dead of night is the toll of a single bell. And I think you'll agree, when I take you up into the bell tower, that none of this is the work of mortal hands.'

The climb to the belfry left Ash breathless. Shaky too, for the last flight of stairs was of old wood and creaky with wear.

'If you'll wait one moment, I'll find the light switch,' said the cleric as he disappeared through a hatch into the bell room itself. 'I'm afraid daylight isn't too good up here.'

When Ash and Kate climbed after him they saw why: the windows were slatted with angled wood, allowing only thin beams of light to penetrate. A single unshaded light bulb was mounted on a crossbeam.

Ash pointed at the heavy bells which were mounted over holes in the floor. 'I see what you mean. No bell ropes.'

'No gongs, Mr Ash. They disappeared long before my time

and no one locally appears to know how or why. And the wheels themselves have long since rusted solid. I'm afraid St Mark's simply doesn't have the resources to make them good again. Nor do my parishioners have the generosity of heart for the finances to be raised.'

He leaned forward and wiped dust from the nearest bell with the palm of his hand.

'So you see, these bells couldn't possibly have rung. Yet one has, more than once recently, loud and clear in the night. To me, it sounded like a death-knell.'

It was early evening when Kate said, 'Why the exception?'

'What?'

She unlocked the door of the Saab. 'You wanted to know the facts beforehand. I wondered why.'

'A feeling, that's all,' Ash replied.

'You suspect "mortal hands" really have been at work here?'

'Come on, Kate. You know that's the cause.'

She smiled. 'That's for you to prove.' The smile hardened. 'David, we didn't talk . . .'

'They're waiting for me. Our vicar and his wife will want me there for Grace.'

'Dinner can wait.'

'No. Now's not the time, Kate. You get yourself back to London, we'll talk when this is over.'

'As usual, you're avoiding the issue.'

'We agreed at the beginning, no full-time commitment. Remember? We both wanted it that way. Christ, after your marriage, I'd have thought you'd be the one to stick to that.'

'Sometimes I forget.' She ducked into the car and started the engine. Before closing the door, and without looking at him, she said, 'Call me later, will you?'

'Kate . . .'

But now the door closed. Her eyes sought his for a single moment, then the Saab pulled away.

Ash watched her go, not angry with himself, but somehow despairing. What the hell did he really want? Why did he always let it fall apart? No, it wasn't that, nothing so definite. He let relationships drift then cool of their own accord, not wanting to hurt, but not wanting to give too much either.

He walked back along the path to the vicarage and found Rev Clemens waiting at the doorstep.

'We're about to start dinner, Mr Ash. Rosemary sent me to fetch you.'

He went into the house with the cleric, almost regretting that he had agreed to stay at the vicarage until the investigation was completed. A room at the local inn might have been preferable, although it made sense to stay near the church itself.

Over dinner the vicar regaled him with stories of Wrexton, of the town's inhabitants and in particular, his own parishioners. He expressed deep regret that St Mark's might well have to be closed down because of all this trouble and that he and his wife would be forced to move to another parish if that were the case. Several times throughout the meal, Ash caught Rosemary – whose consumption of the table wine was even greater than his own – watching him, her eyes not always dropping away immediately. She appeared younger than her husband, although probably by no more than a couple of years. She was plumpish, but by no means unattractive.

It came as a relief when the meal was over and he was able to leave the house to check on the equipment he had set up inside the church, for there was little cheer in Clemens' conversation and Rosemary's eyes had lingered on his own a little longer each time, much to his discomfort.

After the church, Ash phoned Kate from a public call box in the high street. Nothing much to report, he told her; and nothing much to say, he could almost hear her thinking. Talk again tomorrow. If you like. Kate, look, let's get this investigation over with. Of course, David, that's the important thing. I didn't mean . . . I know you didn't; just keep me informed, David. About everything.

After her stiff goodbye Ash made his way to the nearest pub. It was some time later that he returned to the vicarage.

He had been given his own key and he took care not to make too much noise as he climbed the stairs, not wishing to disturb Rev Clemens and his wife at that late hour. He was about to enter his room when he sensed – or perhaps he heard a shifting of weight – someone behind him.

Rosemary Clemens was standing in the doorway opposite, her hand holding closed her unbuttoned nightgown.

'You startled me,' he said.

Her voice was hushed. 'I wanted to apologize for the boredom at dinner.'

He regarded her with some surprise.

'My husband tends to go on about his work and his so-called flock. He can get quite bitter about them, can't he?'

Ash felt awkward standing there, the woman only a few feet away, her hand no longer clutching the nightgown together. He did his best to ignore the shadowed gap. 'There really isn't anything to apologize for.'

She stepped forward. 'Would you like a nightcap? Just one drink? I find it difficult to sleep so early. Unlike Michael.' She indicated with her head a closed door further along the corridor. 'We sleep in separate rooms, David. We have done for years now.'

'It isn't so early,' said Ash. 'It's nearly midnight. And I've got an early start tomorrow.'

'But you'd like a drink, wouldn't you?' She moved even closer to him. 'I'd like to talk to you for a while. Just talk. You don't know what it's like –'

They both became still. And listened to the sonorous toll of the church bell.

Kate huddled in the car, cold and bored. When she had told David two nights before that she felt in need of more 'work in the field' she hadn't imagined herself on stakeout. She blew into her hands to warm them.

Studying St Mark's at this time of night, with its graveyard stretching to the roadside, headstones and tombs sinister shapes in the shadows, she could well believe the place was haunted. The bell tower alone, rising towards the dark rolling clouds, was eerie enough with its deep apertures suggesting the chilly blackness that lay within. She didn't envy David the previous night when he'd had to climb those rickety stairs in the dead of night to discover how the bell was ringing. When he'd entered St Mark's, he had found every item of his detection equipment either smashed or upset. Blood had been smeared over walls and holy pictures. Pews had been overturned. Every candle in the church had been lit.

But he had come upon no intruder.

Not even in the bell tower.

The heavy, single-stroke *clanging* had ceased even before he had entered the church, and when he eventually reached the belfry itself, whoever – or *whatever* – had rung the bell had vanished, leaving behind only more wrecked equipment.

Kate resisted the urge to run the Saab's engine for a short while and use the heater to warm herself up. She sincerely hoped Ash, who was inside the church, having kept the key provided by Rev Clemens, was freezing his butt off! The vicar and his wife thought that he had returned to London to have the spoiled equipment repaired and to collect more, the investigation to be resumed a day or two later. However, Kate herself had driven him back that evening, after he had told her of some interesting gossip he'd picked up in the local pub (the best place of all to learn what was really going on in any town). Even now she was unsure whether or not this was really a matter for the police hereabouts – after all, it *was* a crime that was being committed. But of course, that decision was not for the Institute to make; only the vicar, himself, or his superiors could decide upon that. If Rev Clemens had not been so obsessed with the idea of 'demonic possession', then perhaps the local constabulary would have become involved.

Kate wiped steam from the windscreen, holding her breath so that the glass would remain clear for a few moments. There it was again. There *was* someone out there, someone moving through the graveyard. Using a good deal of stealth, too. And heading for the church.

I hope you haven't fallen asleep, David, Kate said silently to herself. As quietly as possible, she opened the car door.

Ash sat near the back of the darkened church, screened partly by a stone pillar. The only light came from the high stained glass windows each time night clouds slid from the face of the moon. His hands were tucked deep inside his overcoat pockets, lapels crossed over his chest. He shivered. Then heard a sound somewhere in the darkness.

A breeze flickered against his face. A door had been opened.

And there it was, a black form, somehow misshapen, moving among the shadows.

Ash kept still, curious to see what the intruder would do.

A match was struck, the sound harsh in the cavern of the church. A candle was lit. Then another. The figure moved – glided it almost seemed – around the nave, lighting more. That area of the church grew brighter and Ash sank down in his seat, even though he was still in shadow, for now the intruder's true shape was more discernible.

It was bent, as if hunch-backed, and it wore some kind of robe, perhaps a monk's, the head covered by a large cowl.

Ash understood why the figure had appeared crooked, for now it was lifting something. Something heavy.

As Ash watched, the intruder raised the container and began to pour liquid over the altar.

* * *

Kate took the flashlight with her but did not switch it on.

She waited outside the churchyard gate and only when the figure she had been watching had disappeared from view did she enter. Her teeth clenched tight when the gate groaned on its hinges.

She hurried through, not wanting to lose sight of the trespasser for too long, guessing that whoever it was was making for the church's small side door. When gravel crunched under her feet Kate stepped onto the grass verge, taking care not to trip over the stones or grave borders. She was sorely tempted to use the flashlight.

Kate reached the corner of the church and peered round. There was no sign of the person she had been following.

A noise to her right caught her attention. There it was, a shape dodging around headstones. But it was heading away from the church.

Kate's eyes narrowed. That couldn't be right! This person stalking through the cemetery was making for the vicarage itself.

Ash shrank down onto the kneeler below the seat as the cowled figure walked up the centre carrying with it a single candle.

It paused once, looking around as if sensing another presence, and the investigator ducked completely out of sight. He waited, breath held, until the footsteps resumed.

Once they had passed the pew in which he crouched, Ash raised his head to watch. From behind, the hooded figure appeared to have a soft halo, the effect caused by the candle held close to its chest. It went to the narrow doorway leading to the bell tower.

The rising passageway beyond glowed with candlelight as the robed figure began to climb the stone steps, that glow soon diminishing, overwhelmed by the shadow cast. Ash quietly shuffled along the pew, then sped towards the altar where candles that had been removed from their holders now stood burning. Reflections shone from the liquid that had been spilt there.

He took the broad altar steps two at a time, suspecting that the candles had been set in a pool of petrol.

But there were no petrol fumes, although there was an odour. A heavy, unpleasant stench. Ash came to a halt before the altar and touched his fingers to the blood.

'Stop right there.'

Kate switched on the flashlight and shone the beam directly into the man's eyes. She had watched his surreptitious advance on the house, his sly peering through lighted windows, his creeping approach to the back door, her own cover finally broken when she had stumbled over something on the ground. He had spun round, crouching as though expecting to be attacked. Kate had had no other choice than to take the offensive: she blinded him with the light.

'What do you think you're doing?' she demanded to know, hoping the fear in her voice was not noticeable.

'Turn that bloody light off!' came the sharp reply.

No way, thought Kate. 'I asked you a question. Just what the hell are you up to?'

'You mind your own bloody business and get that light out of my face!'

The man took a step towards her and Kate almost turned and ran. We're making enough noise to rouse David, let alone the people inside the house, she reassured herself. Hold tight, don't be intimidated.

The back door of the vicarage opened, light pouring out to hold the trespasser in its full glare.

'What's going on out here?'

Kate recognized the vicar's wife, Rosemary.

'Eric? Is that you?'

The man did not even bother to turn towards her. 'Say nothing, Rosemary.'

The woman in the doorway searched beyond the man she had called Eric, squinting against the dazzle of the flashlight. 'Michael, you said you were meeting with the dean tonight, you said you wouldn't be home 'til very late.'

Kate spoke up, beginning to understand: 'It's you two, isn't it? You're the ones vandalizing the church. My God, that's a sick game to play on your husband, Mrs Clemens.'

'Who is that? Who are you?'

Kate came forward, keeping the flashlight trained on the man as if it were some kind of weapon. 'It's Kate McCarrick, Mrs Clemens. From the Psychical Research Institute. I was with David Ash yesterday.'

'But . . . but what are you doing here?' One hand gripped the doorframe as though for support.

'What you get up to outside your marriage is your own business,' said Kate, coming into the light from the doorway. 'Although, God knows, your affairs appear to be common knowledge in the town. But to turn your own husband into a nervous wreck by desecrating his church is a bit rich.' She turned off the flashlight and the man wiped a hand across his eyes with relief. 'Why torment your husband that way, Mrs Clemens? What did you hope to achieve?'

'She's mad,' said the man called Eric, scowling at Kate. 'You're bloody mad, woman,' he repeated.

'I think you've both got a lot of explaining to do,' Kate replied calmly. 'The police don't take kindly to –'

She stopped speaking. All three of them turned towards the grey looming church from where, once again, there came the steady tolling of a bell.

Ash ascended the stone steps of the tower, the ponderous ringing of the bell seeming to draw him onwards, the spiralling noise almost deafening in the confines of the stairway. Up he went, flashlight held before him to light the way, his breathing becoming laboured, legs already beginning to ache with the effort.

He stumbled, grazing his shin against stone; but he quickly went on, determined to find out (although his suspicions were undeniably strong) just who was 'haunting' St Mark's. There was something very wrong about this place of worship, something unhealthy he could not help but feel, but it had nothing to do with demons. The rottenness – he could think of no better term – had more to do with the weakness of human nature than ghostly sacrilege. The parishioners were turning away from the Rev Clemens' church for reasons other than its or their own spiritual decline.

When he reached the second level, Ash rested against the wall to catch his breath, the flashlight off and dropped to his side. From here on, the stairs were wooden and creaky: he would have to time his steps so that they coincided with the ringing of the bell and its after-tones. Above he could see the faint candle-glow through the hatchway and the rope holes in the rough floorboards.

Ash waited no more than a few seconds before continuing the journey, apprehensive now, the deafening noise increasing his edginess.

The fluttering light from above was abruptly cut out as though someone was deliberately shielding the candle. Ash advanced slowly, one hand touching the stairs ahead of him for support. He reached the hatchway, but crouched cautiously as he took a further step so that only the top half of his head was inside the belfry itself. The shadow of the hooded figure was huge against the far wall.

Ash faced the kneeling intruder as he rose through the hatchway, the other person's back to him. The robed figure was busy with something by the wall.

Still the bell chimed, its thunderous sound almost unbearable. Yet none of the bells was moving. Nor was the figure close enough to strike any.

'*Turn it off!*' Ash shouted, unable to stand the dreadful

noise any longer. The other person did not appear to hear him.

Ash clambered into the belfry, enraged rather than apprehensive now.

'*Turn it off!*' he screamed, and this time he switched on the flashlight, pointing it at the kneeling figure.

Whoever it was there stiffened, became very still for a moment or two. Then the figure began to turn.

Ash held the flashlight at arm's length, like an aimed gun.

There could have been a void inside the cowl so deeply black was it before the light struck. A face gradually came into view.

'Turn it off.' On this third occasion, Ash spoke the command, knowing it would not be heard anyway over the clamour. He was quite prepared to knock the crouched figure aside and kick the machine into submission, so maddeningly loud was the amplification within the confines of the belfry. But the vicar understood Ash's words even if he did not hear them. He reached behind him and flicked a switch.

The relief was instant, although the resonance in the atmosphere took time to fade.

'Let them sort it out,' Ash said as he and Kate McCarrick walked through the graveyard towards the Saab. 'We've done our job, the rest is up to them.' The vicarage door behind them was being quietly closed by the rural dean's assistant, while the dean himself was gently talking to the Rev Clemens inside the house.

'The Institute's report won't help him at all,' said Kate. She felt depressed, not because the case had fizzled to nothing more than human frailty, but because she had sympathy for the vicar himself.

'Not our problem,' Ash replied uncompromisingly. 'He should have gone to his superiors and asked for their help.'

'The fact that he suspected his wife of sleeping with half

the men in town might have been a difficult subject for a vicar to broach.'

Ash shrugged. 'Not half the men. But enough to feed the gossip. I think he hated his parishioners for their tittle-tattle more than he hated his wife.'

'But to fake a possession . . .'

'He wanted St Mark's closed down. He wanted to leave this area and start afresh. Who can blame him for that?'

Kate opened the driver's door as Ash walked around to the other side. He climbed in and ran his hands down his face. 'I'm beat,' he said.

'Don't sleep on the way back. I need company this time of night.' Kate checked the dashboard clock. 'Morning, I mean.' She closed the car door. 'Did you know all along?'

He shook his head wearily. 'I suspected. He was so bloody neurotic to begin with. No point now having the blood on the altar cloth analysed, but I bet we'd find it belonged to an animal. There are probably the carcasses of a few stray dogs or cats – maybe even sheep – hidden in the fields around here, or floating down the local river.'

'That's horrible. He was a man of God.'

'Driven to the limits. Could be he was a little bit crazy anyway. Who can say if it was *all* Rosemary's fault? The thing that interested me was how he did it.' Ash drew out a pack of cigarettes and lit one. 'The blood, the candles, the fires, the wreckage – all that was easy enough for someone who had access to the church. The outrage was meant to look diabolical, but when you think about it, no serious damage was ever done. If he'd flipped completely, or if his own holy vows hadn't held him in check, he could have burned down the place. But what I wanted to know was how he'd rigged the bell.'

'A simple timer device fixed to a tape recorder.'

'Right. He didn't have a chance to set it today because he'd spent most of his time with the dean.'

Kate turned the ignition key and the Saab gunned into life. 'Rosemary thought he would be at the dean's most of the night. She thought the way was clear for her latest lover.'

'The reverend made his excuses and left early, thinking I was safely back in London. It was all so stupid though – I'd have found the tape recorder hidden behind the boards sooner or later, even if I'd had to tear the belfry apart.'

'I suppose reason didn't have much to do with it.'

Ash drew on the cigarette, relaxing back in the passenger seat. 'It didn't make for much of a challenge either. It was all so obvious. There's only one little thing that still bothers me, though,' he added.

Kate glanced at him questioningly.

'Two days ago, when I first went inside St Mark's, I saw someone by the altar. Someone who was either kneeling, or was quite small. I think now that maybe it was a child.

'I assumed that person had left by the side door, but when we all examined that same door only minutes later, it was locked and bolted from the inside. Yet there was no way that anyone could have got past us unseen, and no way they could have left through there.'

Kate joined him in looking back across the graveyard at the church.

T E N

Steam curled to brush the ceiling in delicate licks, its ascent stippling the white tiles of the bathroom walls with moisture. The only sound was that of water splashing, the movement vigorous, the cleansing that was taking place more than a physical purification: Ash scrubbed at his flesh as if to scour what lay beneath, feeling that in some way the filth from the pond had tainted his inner self. An irrational notion, but one he could not easily exorcize.

The dirt soon washed away; the sense of defilement did not.

The bath was huge, the enamel stained deep brown beneath old upright taps, its clawed feet squat, as if cowered under the great weight. A small mirror above a solidly square sink was misted opaque; a pale green stool stood by the bath, paintwork cracked, flaked away in places.

He finally rose from the water, dark hair on face and body matted flat against his skin. His fingers wiped the wetness from his eyes, the flat of his hands scratching against the roughness of his chin. He stepped from the bath and reached for a large towel hanging over a rail behind the door, careful not to slip on the shiny floor. Ash dried himself briskly, starting with his face and hair, working down, the towel rough against his skin, the wiping still part of the cleansing process. At one point he stopped, listened, looked towards the bathroom door. But he heard nothing, and felt only the stillness of Edbrook itself. He resumed drying himself, then pulled on a robe, his body now damp from the steam that had accumulated.

Ash yanked the bath plug and used a hand to wash away the dirt mark that was left as the water level lowered. He watched the whirlpool over the drain as though mesmerized; but his thoughts were elsewhere, in another time, caught in a more powerful vortex . . . He shuddered, became aware of the present once more. Ash breathed in deeply, vapoured air rushing into his throat; he released it in a long sigh, forcing his fluttering nerves to settle.

The last of the water gurgled away and Ash went to the bathroom door, finding its brass handle slippery, difficult to grip. He hesitated before tightening his hold and twisting, wondering why he should feel that someone waited beyond as he did so. Coolness rushed in at him from the dim but empty corridor.

Running his hands through his wet hair, Ash returned barefooted to his bedroom, tiredness, despite his tension, almost overwhelming.

He closed the door behind him and went to the bureau where his notes and plans of the house were spread. By them there was now a tumbler glass and he quickly poured a generous measure of vodka into it. He took a large swallow, then another, waiting for the warmness to reach his chest, the initial lightness to glide into his head, before approaching the window. He stared down into the gardens, relieved that the terrace and pond were not in view from that part of the house.

He disliked the statues out there, and the shadows cast by single trees and shrubbery. Could he be *sure* that's all they were? What the hell was the matter with him? He'd fallen into the pond, pushed by someone – some*one*, not a dog! – and had thought, *imagined*, that person had been in the water with him, had wanted him drowned. But that fleeting image was jumbled, confused by events of many years before, a terrible memory creating its own falsehood. Damn it! He had to calm himself, he had to think logically! There was a secretiveness about the Mariells; he sensed they were holding something back from him. Idiot! He had *told* them not to divulge anything, not at this preliminary stage of the investigation. He was allowing just one unnerving experience to distort everything else. The family genuinely believed they were being haunted; he considered it his task to dissuade them from that by providing firm evidence to the contrary, to explain rationally the disturbance – in whatever shape or form it took – at Edbrook. Ghosts, spirits, lost souls, did not, *could* not exist. In a day or two – hopefully less – they'd be convinced. And he, himself, would be certain again.

Disgustedly, he turned away from the window and crossed the room to the bed, taking the vodka bottle and tumbler with him. He placed them on the bedside cabinet where they would be close at hand, shrugged off the robe, and climbed into bed.

The coldness of the sheets made him shiver. The smothered moon afforded no light when he switched off the bedside lamp. His eyes remained open. He stared up at the dark grey mass that was the ceiling . . .

No lights, no glow from within. Edbrook was a vast black bulk that merged with the blackness of night clouds. A breeze stirred through the gardens, ruffling foliage, disturbing trees. In the woods, night creatures hunted, their skirmishes violent but brief. Honey fungus glowed blue-green on decaying tree trunks, beetles scuttled in the undergrowth. The moon was a pale ghost seen only behind slow-moving monoliths.

Inside the house, Ash slept; but he did not rest.

His dream was of water, a terrible churning pressure all around him. Occasionally his eyes would rise above its choppy surface and he would glimpse the riverbanks on either side, far out of reach and rushing away from him. He screamed and cold liquid filled his mouth; and that choking sensation was familiar to him.

He plunged, drawn down by the fierce undertow. Someone else was with him in the deep, a blurred image, struggling as was he. Her hair was wild around her face, her arms and legs flailed the water. Her mouth, too, was open as though she was screaming at the horror of what was happening to them. The girl was drifting away from him, her figure becoming even more unclear, softened and bedimmed by the coursing river; yet still, and peculiarly, he noticed her white ankle-sock, one shoe missing. Then she was gone, lost in fluid mists.

He rose again, a boy too feeble to defend himself against the water's violence, but light enough in weight to be tossed upwards like flotsam by the currents.

He saw her once more, but her hand only, a small pale beacon that appeared to wave before it was sucked down, the young girl claimed completely . . .

Ash awoke, his cry little more than a whimper. The terror of his nightmare remained in his wide eyes. And soon a different emotion tinged them: a deep sadness, perhaps remorse. His flesh was coldly damp.

Early-morning light crept through the window, a seeping greyness that offered no cheer.

E L E V E N

Ash knelt to examine the fine powder at the top of the stairs. Too many footsteps had disturbed it, either last night or that morning – probably both – for it to reveal anything of use. He scooped up some, then stood. He let the powder drift to the floor again, looking for signs of draughts; there were no diversions in its floating descent. He checked the thermometer nearby. A low reading, but certainly not as low as the previous night's, and quite normal for a morning at that time of year.

Ash went downstairs and followed the murmur of voices into the breakfast room. Christina was giggling at something that Simon was saying, while Robert Mariell, at the head of the table, was smiling at them both. Conversation ceased when the investigator entered the room.

'Mr Ash,' Robert welcomed, indicating a seat next to Nanny Tess and opposite his younger brother and sister. 'I hope you managed to sleep after your nasty little accident last night.'

Ash pulled back the chair and sat. 'Uh, yes . . . I slept,' he replied. 'I still don't understand what happened though. I'm sure – I'm *positive* – I saw a girl outside.'

They regarded him in silence.

'All right,' he admitted, 'maybe it was the dog who knocked

me into the pond – I'm too confused about that to insist otherwise. But I know I followed the figure of a person from the house and I'm sure it was a girl.' He looked across the table. 'I thought it was you, Christina.'

She returned his gaze, but said nothing.

It was Simon who broke the silence. 'I really do think it's time we told our investigator what's been going on here at Edbrook.'

After a moment's hesitation, Robert agreed. 'Yes, of course. We refrained from doing so last night because you were somewhat distraught, and because your own instructions were that we should give nothing away for the present. However, I feel it's time we spoke of our haunting.'

Ash nodded. 'It's time.'

'Well then, it's fair that Nanny should start. She was the first to be confronted by our ghost.'

All eyes turned towards the aunt, who had left the table to fetch Ash's breakfast. She laid the plate before him (a meagre portion of scrambled eggs, bacon, and mushrooms), and sat, casting her eyes down at her own half-eaten breakfast as if reluctant to speak.

'Come along, Nanny, don't be shy,' Simon encouraged. 'Mr Ash is here to help us.'

Ash's urging was more gentle. 'Tell me what you experienced, Miss Webb. I won't be surprised at anything you say.'

Still she was reluctant, her voice faltering. 'I . . . I've seen . . . the ghost a few times.'

'In the same place?' he asked.

'No. In various parts of the house. And . . . and in the garden.'

'By the pond?'

She avoided his eyes. 'Yes. Once.'

Ash glanced around at the others, his face grim. 'What form does it take?' he asked, his attention returning to the aunt. 'What does this apparition – this ghost – look like?'

'It's a girl,' she answered. 'A young girl.'

Ash caught the secretive smile that passed between Simon

and Christina. He hid his annoyance. 'Dressed in a white flowing gown of some sort, possibly a nightgown,' he said, not as a question.

Nanny Tess nodded, her discomfort apparent.

'Over what period of time?'

She looked up at him. 'I'm sorry?'

'How long have you been witnessing the phenomenon?'

'Ghost, surely, Mr Ash,' Robert Mariell interrupted.

'That hasn't been established yet,' Ash replied curtly. 'How long, Miss Webb?'

'Years,' she said. 'It must be years.'

'Then why is it only now that you want the matter investigated?'

Robert spoke up for her again. 'Ah, because until recently it was only Nanny who bore witness to the, uh, "phenomenon". Now we all have.'

Simon's hand went to his mouth as he tried to suppress a giggle.

Ash stared at him. 'Is this some kind of joke?'

'You must forgive my brother,' apologized Robert. 'He tends to find humour in most situations.'

'I'm not alone in that,' Simon quickly responded.

The older Mariell ignored him.

'You're being extremely rude to our guest,' Nanny Tess scolded.

'You're quite right, of course, Nanny,' Robert said, smiling. He turned to the investigator. 'I'm afraid Nanny Tess has suffered our juvenile humour since we were children. I often wonder why she's put up with us for so long.'

Quietly, almost to herself, the aunt said, 'Somebody had to. Somebody . . .' Once again her head bowed as if she were studying the plate before her, the food there hardly touched.

Ash made an attempt to begin his own breakfast, though he had scant appetite. 'You said you've all now seen what you believe to be the ghost of a girl.'

Robert answered for them. 'More than once. And each of

us in different parts of the house. But only Nanny has seen this poor spirit beyond the walls of Edbrook.'

'What makes you say "poor" spirit?'

'Isn't that what these apparitions are – the desolate souls of those unfortunates who have left their earthly bodies in traumatic, or perhaps even tragic circumstances? I'm sure I read that somewhere.'

'It's an accepted theory.'

For the first time that morning, Christina spoke up: 'But not accepted by you.'

Light from the long windows behind her, as the day at last began to brighten, haloed her hair a deep glowing red. There was a hint of amusement in her eyes – something else that Ash was quickly becoming used to – and he wondered if she were mocking him. 'I'm prepared to believe that emotions of certain distressed people can be so strong at the moment of death, whether through pain, unhappiness, or shock, that an impression is left behind. An after-image, if you like, that can take years, maybe centuries, to fade completely.' He turned from Christina to Robert. 'I imagine Edbrook has quite a history. Has the Mariell family always owned the property?'

'Many, many generations of the Mariells have lived here, Mr Ash,' Robert told him. 'Since it was built in the 16th century, in fact.'

'Then you might know –'

The other man was quick to interrupt. 'The Mariells have always preferred to forget their misfortunes. As far as I'm aware, no Edbrook tragedies have been recorded. Our generation has its own, of course – the death of our parents when we were only children – but that was due to an accident far from here.'

'No guests, no servants, ever died in unfortunate circumstances inside the house?'

'Ah, those were the days when there were servants at Edbrook. Now the running of the house falls entirely on the shoulders of poor Nanny. She copes very well . . .'

The aunt, who was pouring tea for their guest, didn't appear to appreciate the compliment. Ash thanked her when she placed the cup before him and was puzzled by her taciturnity.

'But I've no knowledge,' her nephew continued, 'of murders or suicides of either guests or servants in Edbrook's history.'

'With a house this old it'd be a little unusual if there wasn't a skeleton or two lurking in a cupboard somewhere.' He added milk to his tea, then sipped it before saying, 'It would help to know who the girl was.'

Christina leaned forward, her hands resting on the table. 'Then you believe a ghost does haunt this house.'

He shrugged. 'There may be a visual representation of someone who once lived here still lingering. Perhaps that's what I saw last night. A manifestation of some kind.'

'Surely that's just a fancy term for "ghost",' Simon insisted somewhat scornfully.

'No, just another word for "image". It doesn't have to be a ghost in the sense you mean.' He looked around the table. 'Later this morning, I'd like each of you –'

A small cry came from Nanny Tess. In her hand she held the pepper pot, the top of which, along with a mound of pepper, now lay on her breakfast plate. Simon and Christina burst into laughter and when their aunt started sneezing, that laughter became uproarious. Even Robert started to chuckle.

Ash looked from face to face, perplexed by the childish trick.

His eyes rested on Christina and through her laughter she noticed his study. Her merriment faded. She looked to her brothers as if for reassurance, but they did not seem to notice.

Ash continued to watch her, but she avoided his eyes. He wondered why.

T W E L V E

Kate McCarrick pushed through the swing doors of the Psychical Research Institute and strode across to the reception desk, bidding its occupant good morning and collecting a pile of letters and packages from her. She sorted through them as she made her way upstairs to her office, murmuring hello to colleagues she passed on the way.

Once inside her own room, she dumped the correspondence on her desk, then took off scarf and coat to hang them behind the door. Settled, she flicked through her appointments diary, lifting the telephone receiver with her other hand and pressing the O button as she did so.

'Jenny, has David Ash tried to reach me this morning?' she asked. 'No? Get a number for me then, will you?' After giving the Mariell name and their home address, Kate replaced the receiver. She began opening her post.

At the same time, in the library of Edbrook, David Ash was re-positioning a Polaroid camera and its tripod, careful not to dislodge the wires connected to other sensor equipment.

Robert Mariell, hands clasped behind his back, watched in what might have been amused silence.

'About here?' asked the investigator, looking towards the observer for confirmation.

'Yes, there at first, and then . . .' Robert waved his hand nonchalantly around the room '. . . here, there . . . several places, actually.'

Ash straightened up, satisfied at least that the camera covered a good portion of the library. 'Has she ever spoken? Have you tried to speak to her?'

Robert frowned. 'My dear chap, I don't make a habit of conducting conversations with ghosts. I consider just seeing the wretched thing queer enough.' He twitched his shoulders in a shiver. 'At any rate, your camera seems to be in a good enough position to catch anything. Tell me what all this nonsense that it's attached to is.'

Ash pointed. 'That's called a capacitance change detector. Any movement in the room and it'll trigger off the camera and the tape recorder. I'll set it later when we're sure none of us is likely to enter the library.' He reached into his jacket and produced a micro-tape recorder. 'I'd like you to tell me exactly what you saw. For the record.'

Robert's eyebrows arched. 'For the record?'

'For the Institute's files only. Complete confidentiality guaranteed.' He switched on the tiny machine and placed it on the corner of a table between himself and the other man.

Robert studied it for a moment or two before speaking. 'Very well,' he said at last. 'I saw a girl in this room, although she was only a hazy sort of form at first, not clear at all. Definitely a girl though, in her early twenties, I'd say. I saw her – it – again a few days – no, not days: *nights* – later, much clearer this time, almost as if her presence was growing in strength. I must admit, I felt quite weak at the sight of her.'

'That sometimes happens. Manifestations of this kind seem to draw off psychic energy from their witnesses, using it to strengthen their own form. They're able to sap energy from the atmosphere too – that's why the temperature of a room may suddenly drop. Their presence has even been known to affect electricity.'

'Extraordinary. But you really are speaking of ghosts, Mr Ash.'

'No, I'm still talking about unexplained phenomena. Please go on with what you were telling me.'

Robert began to pace, then remembered the tape recorder lying on the table. He returned to his original position. 'I felt there was something terribly sad about this . . . this "presence" . . . as though she were searching, or perhaps just lost . . .'

The small tape spools turned slowly, absorbing the sounds of the room, catching even the movement of feet on the wood-block floor, the flaring of a match struck by the investigator to light his cigarette.

Kate left the filing cabinet drawer half-open as she went back to her desk to answer the phone.

'McCarrick,' she said, then frowned at the buzz of Jenny's voice on the line. 'There has to be a number,' Kate insisted. 'Did you enquire if it was ex-directory?'

She listened.

'Not listed? That can't be right.' She paused to think. 'Okay, Jenny, thanks for trying.'

Kate replaced the receiver and drummed the desk top with the fingers of one hand, lost in thought.

The tape recorder was a reel-to-reel, and although not micro, small enough to be easily portable. It was connected to a vibration detector. Simon Mariell watched with interest as the psychic investigator placed the machine and its attachment on a low shelf in the cellar of Edbrook. Set close by on a tripod was a time-lapse camera fitted with an electronic flash unit, which was covered with a filter that would only pass infra-red radiation. The camera used black and white IR film, and was triggered by an in-built IR detector that would sense a person's presence.

The dankness of the underground chamber was unpleasant, the musty smell an irritant, but Ash ignored the discomfort as he reached for a large greenhouse thermometer and hung it from a wine rack. The single low-wattage light bulb used to illuminate what was a considerable area threw deep shadows into the furthest recesses and alcoves. He slapped his hands together to dislodge dust and turned to the other man.

'Didn't your paraphernalia catch anything last night?' Simon asked.

'I didn't set up anything down here.'

'But the rest of the house?'

'Not a thing. Still, I hadn't worked out precise locations for any of the equipment.'

'Perhaps you should have asked us for more details then.'

'That wasn't the idea. I wanted to see what I could come up with myself first.'

Simon grinned. 'It appears you came up with a bit more than you bargained for.' He dug his hands into his trouser pockets, seeming to enjoy the moment. 'So what do you want me to tell you? How I came face to face with the phantom lady down here in the cellar?'

'I'd be interested to hear. Tell me something else first: How old was your mother when she died?'

Simon smiled at the question, not in the least perturbed. 'A lot older than our vision, my friend. I think that's a tree you needn't bark up.'

'How did Christina react?'

'To our parents' deaths? My God, just like the rest of us – she was devastated! What would you expect? We were very young. It was fortunate that we had someone like Nanny Tess around to take care of us.'

There was a small satisfaction for Ash in that he had finally managed to wipe the smirk from Simon's face. The other man shifted uncomfortably, annoyance at his interrogator plainly evident.

'Look, I'd rather talk about our haunting, if you don't mind,' Simon told him almost petulantly. 'This cellar is damp and rather unpleasant.'

'I'm sorry,' Ash apologized, bringing out the micro-recorder and clicking it on. 'Please go ahead and tell me exactly what you saw down here.'

Still irritable, Simon replied: 'The same as the others. A girl. I've seen her lurking or hovering or whatever these bloody things do on several occasions. That first time, I'd come down for some wine and there she was, over there watching me.' He pointed and shuddered as if for emphasis. 'The sight made my blood run cold, I can tell you.'

'Does she look like anyone you know? Have known?'

'Of course not. In fact, that's the horrible part of this affair.' His features contorted in disgust. 'There was something wrong with her face, her figure . . . something awful. She appeared . . . I don't know – *malformed* . . . in some way.'

Ash moved forward with the recorder to catch Simon Mariell's words.

While in the hall above, Nanny Tess leaned closer to the half-open door to listen.

T H I R T E E N

Kate looked up from the typewriter as her office door opened, the reading glasses she wore balanced precariously on the end of her nose. Edith Phipps peered round the door as if she were hesitant to enter. Her face was anxious.

'You said you'd call me . . .' There was anxiety in the medium's voice, too.

'Yes, I'm sorry,' Kate said, waving a hand for Edith to come in. 'But there's nothing to report, I'm afraid. It's weird, but the Mariell household doesn't appear to have a phone.'

The medium took a seat opposite the Institute's director, her eyes intent on Kate's. 'Hasn't David been in touch with you yet?'

Kate smiled placatingly. 'No, and there's nothing unusual in that. He's a great one for disappearing without trace for days on end. David sometimes becomes so involved in an investigation he forgets he's responsible to anyone.' She removed her glasses and rested back in the chair. 'Anyhow, if they're not on the phone, I don't see how he could get in touch, unless he were to call from somewhere outside. Remember though, he's without a car – I can't imagine him trudging through country lanes to get to a phone box, can you?' She smiled again to add lightness to her words.

It had little effect: Edith's face was pale. 'The house is that remote?' the medium said.

'According to the letters I received it's a couple of miles from the nearest village. That's why Miss Webb arranged to pick David up at the station.' Kate became serious. She had felt uneasy about Edith's phone call the night before, but the cold light of day had provided some reality to the situation: it was foolish in the extreme to be apprehensive over one day's loss of contact with David. Although Edith Phipps was a well-regarded psychic, she was not beyond mistakes. No medium was infallible; far from it. Nevertheless, Kate was still sympathetic towards her colleague's distress. 'Are you still really that concerned, Edith?' she asked, her voice softening.

The medium clasped her hands together, shaking them in her lap. 'The feeling that he was in danger was so intense last night . . .'

'Yes, I admit you had me worried, too. But all we can do is wait until we hear from him. He's experienced enough to take care of himself, you know.'

Edith flushed, apology in her expression. 'You think I'm being a silly old woman.'

'I'm too impressed with your sensory ability ever to think that,' Kate replied soothingly. 'I'm only asking you to be practical; there's very little we can do until David gets in touch. Let's be patient a while longer.'

But her smile this time was less than confident.

FOURTEEN

The day had changed, from dull to bright, from bright to brilliant autumnal glory, a sunny remission before winter took firm, disheartening hold. The air remained chill, but its bite had freshness, its breath had vigour.

They walked through the shaded woods, Christina and Ash, occasionally breaking through to clearings that were alive with russet colours, stopping when a small startled animal scurried invisibly through beds of fallen leaves at their approach, pausing to watch a grey squirrel defy gravity as it leapt from bough to bough. In a denser part of the woods, Christina, who had taken the lead, laughed like a child when she allowed a thin branch to whip back against Ash's chest. Surprised, but not hurt, he chuckled at her delighted face as she turned to him.

Christina ran on ahead, urging him to keep up with her, chastising him for his 'decrepit' slowness. He watched her scramble up a steep incline, using tufts of grass and exposed tree roots to pull herself onwards, her long skirt lifting to reveal slim calves and fine-boned ankles. His mood lightened, perhaps because he was away from the cloying gloom of the house, and partly because her blitheness was infectious.

He slipped as he tried to follow her, sliding back down to

the level ground in a flurry of leaves and trickling earth, and this delighted her even more. Christina's laughter rang through the forest.

He wiped himself down, grinning ruefully, tenseness from the previous night finally lifting. Ash attempted the climb once more, and made it this time, Christina taunting him good-humouredly all the way.

They walked on, enjoying each other's company, hardly talking, feeling little need to.

After a while, they rested in a glade, shielded by trees from any breeze, warmed by shafts of sunlight. Ash leaned back against the broad trunk of an oak, somewhat breathless, his eyes closed, face upturned towards the sun. Christina sat close by, legs curled under her, one hand resting in the grass.

'I'm more out of condition than I thought,' he said, brushing a tickling insect from his cheek. 'I feel as though I've run a mile in lead shoes.'

'The penalty of city life,' she said in reply.

'All that debauchery; it was bound to catch up.' He reached into his coat pocket for the micro-recorder. 'D'you mind this while we talk?'

She shook her head and seemed amused by the small machine. 'I don't mind at all. What did you want to talk about?' Her question was almost teasing.

'About you, your brothers. The house.'

She laughed lightly. 'That's interesting enough to record?'

'It could be.'

Christina opened her hands. 'Where do I start?'

He switched on the tape. 'Tell me where you've seen the ghost.'

'So you're now calling what we saw a ghost?'

'Only to simplify matters. The difference isn't important at this stage.'

'Why are you such a sceptic?' She appeared genuinely puzzled.

'I prefer to think of myself as a realist,' he answered her.

She pondered on this for a moment or two, then said: 'I've

seen her in the hallway. In the corridors. I've seen her in your room. Once, when I was in the garden, I noticed her watching me from a window.'

'And she's never communicated with you?'

Her voice was quiet. 'I think she wants to. I think she's desperate to. It's as if she hasn't the power, she can only appear, no more than that.'

'Does she frighten you?'

Christina gave a small shake of her head. 'No, she makes me sad. She seems . . . so lost.'

Ash took time to consider. 'How did your parents die, Christina?'

It was as if a shadow had passed over her face, and perhaps one had, the tops of trees shifting across the sunlight, blown by a sudden wind.

'It was so long ago,' she said, and he could see the anguish was still there inside her, suppressed but close enough to the surface for others to be aware of its presence. 'They'd left us in the care of Nanny Tess – she's Mother's younger sister. I think my mother loved to enjoy life too much to be shackled by children, so my aunt was a nanny to us even before my parents were killed.'

'You were just kids when it happened?'

'We were very young.'

A leaf dropped lazily between them, its edges curled and brown. Another followed. Ash felt the ground's coldness seeping into him, despite the sun's warm rays.

'But you asked me how they died,' said Christina. 'It was a motoring accident. They were driving through France, on their way to visit friends in Dijon when it happened. Nobody knows how or why, but apparently their car just ran off the road. Nobody was even sure who'd been driving – their car burst into flames. All that was found inside were two . . . were two charred . . . bodies . . . burnt beyond recognition . . .'

He switched off the recorder and leaned towards her to touch her arm. 'I'm sorry,' he said. 'I didn't mean to dredge up such bad memories.'

'It was so long ago – it's only a distant thought now, reality hardly plays a part.'

'You must have missed them terribly.'

'We were fortunate to have Nanny Tess. And fortunate, too, that there was enough money left to provide for us.'

'Miss Webb was trustee?'

Christina nodded. 'Nanny has kept the family together all these years, even though we must have driven her near to breaking point at times.'

Abruptly her mood changed. She laughed at Ash's quizzical expression.

'Our games,' she explained. 'From the time we were little we've always loved to tease, to play tricks on each other. Nanny says we inherited it from Mother – she sometimes used to drive Father frantic with her games. Just as we do with Nanny.'

'Yeah, I noticed at breakfast,' he said drily. 'Doesn't she ever get mad at you?'

Again she laughed, a light sound, but full of mischief. 'Frequently. But she's learned to accept us for what we are.' She pulled at a blade of grass, played its tip along her lips. 'She scolded us more when we were children, and that was mainly because we could be particularly spiteful to one another – you know how children are. I was probably worse than Robert or Simon, but then what would you expect of a girl with two older brothers?'

'You don't have to tell me how spiteful sweet little girls can be.'

Christina regarded him curiously. 'You said that as someone who knows from bitter experience.'

He looked away. 'I, uh, I had a sister myself.'

'Had?'

He stared into the distance. 'Juliet. She . . .' it was as if he found the word difficult to say '. . . drowned . . . when we were kids. We both fell into a river, but I was the lucky one – I was pulled clear.' He remembered the small pale hand

107

disappearing beneath the water's surface. Its fingers had been outstretched.

Now Christina reached forward and gently touched his hand. He was startled.

'Are you still afraid of water?' she asked him softly. 'Is that why you panicked so last night?'

He didn't answer, but searched her eyes, her hand still upon his. He turned away again, unsure, flustered.

'I'm confused about what happened,' he said at last. 'But I still have nightmares about Juliet's death. Maybe they got confused with reality last night.' He thought of arms pulling him from the water; but was it a memory of hours, or years before?

'You still think of Juliet,' she quietly prompted.

His reply was cold. 'I can barely remember her.'

He fumbled in his pockets for cigarettes, drew them out. One was in his mouth before he remembered to offer the pack to Christina. She shook her head, watching him. Ash flicked on his lighter, inhaled smoke. He was about to say more, the flame still alight, half-forgotten, when he noticed her staring at his raised hand. She was gazing at the tiny spear of fire as though fascinated.

She blinked when he snuffed the flame.

And then she was on her feet, brushing creases from her long skirt with her hands. 'We should get back to the house,' she told him.

Bemused, Ash stayed where he was.

'Bet I can get back before you!' Christina taunted. With a laugh, she whirled and ran off into the trees.

Ash stubbed his unsmoked cigarette into the earth and scrambled to his feet. He called after her. 'Hey, not so fast! I'll get lost!' But Christina ignored him and he could only watch resignedly as her figure moved further away.

He stalked off in her wake, not quite sure if he were irritated or amused by her childishness. The loss of their parents at such a tender age had hardly matured Christina and her brother Simon; but then perhaps that was what they lacked – the firm hand of a father, the steadying influence of a mother. Nanny Tess obviously hadn't fulfilled either role. Robert appeared to be the patriarch figure, although his manner was one of benevolent aloofness.

He caught glimpses of Christina ahead of him, a bright shape flitting through the trees.

'Christina! Give me a break . . .' he shouted, but heard only her distant laughter.

The woods were hushed, the trudging of his own footsteps through fallen leaves the loudest sound. And soon he had lost sight of Christina altogether.

He stopped. Looked around. Had he heard someone behind him? He called her name again.

There was no reply, not even her laughter now.

He walked on, only to stop once more.

Had a figure ducked behind a tree to his left?

He waited a moment, but there was no more movement. He continued, becoming annoyed with the silly game.

The noise that brought him to a halt this time was different. It had sounded like a child's giggle.

He whirled and caught a fleeting glimpse of something hurry through the trees to his right. But it was gone in an eye's blink.

Ridiculously, he thought it might have been a small girl. It had moved so fast, though. He couldn't be sure.

He turned his head, sharply. No, he couldn't have heard the whisper of voices; surely the muted sounds had been a breeze sighing through the woods.

Now the faintest echo of laughter.

Ash drew in a shallow breath. A feeling was rising – was *creeping* – from the hollow of his stomach – or so it seemed – spreading upwards and outwards, a gradual sensory frosting of sinews and nerve lines, seeping through to his outer skin, prickling its surface with tiny bumps. An unease that he could not understand; yet a sensing which he could not ignore. His pace quickened as he walked on through the forest.

Occasionally he would look behind him. Sometimes he

would glance sharply to his right, other times to his left. He was not alone. Yet there was no one else with him.

Ash did not run. But he walked in haste.

He heard a snigger, he felt the touch of a hand on his shoulder. The touch could only have been the brushing of leaves. But the snigger could not have been anything else but a snigger.

He almost stumbled, his hand scraping across the rough bark of a tree. He did not linger.

The woods seemed more shaded, more gloomy, as if dusk were impossibly premature. The coldness might well have been in his own mind, for he could feel perspiration on his brow, the clinging of his shirt, the dampness against his lower back. He hurried, now ignoring the small noises that seemed to keep pace with him, the shadows that had no substance when focused upon.

And then he was in bright sunshine, the clearing he had burst into summer warm, as though it had trapped and stored its own heat. He even heard the lazy drone of a blowfly which had found sanctuary from the season's death-chill. His eyes narrowed against the unexpected glare.

The clearing was an orderless area of coarse grass and foliage, with several openings that could have been paths around its ragged fringes. At the centre, its stone walls lichen-patched and stained, stood a small, square edifice. Its door, a tall rusted iron gate with grass growing through the lower bars, was ajar. Two earthenware vases filled with wilted flowers were on either side of the entrance.

He realized that the building, neglected and weather-worn, could only be a mausoleum. A tomb. The previous Mariells' final resting place?

Curious, he moved closer.

The sun slowly drew the coolness from his body.

There came a sound from within the tomb. A shifting.

Ash paused, the long grass steadying to a rest in his wake.

'Christina, is that you?'

He waited for a reply. There was none. But there was another sound from within the shadowed entrance.

He forced good humour. 'Okay, Christina, joke's over. You've had your fun.'

The silence was not comforting.

Weary of the game, he sighed. 'Christina . . .'

The air itself seemed strangely still. Ash stepped closer to the old building and his hand reached in for the gate, fingers curling around a bar as if for support. He noticed at the side of the entrance a plaque, grimed with age, muddied by passing seasons. At the top he could just discern parts of the Mariell name.

He pushed at the gate and it scraped noisily on its hinges as it swung stiffly inwards. Inside, the air was dank, stale, and there came to him a sense of total emptiness. Yet there were tiers in there, narrow concrete platforms set against the walls. On them were stone coffins.

His voice was very quiet when he said, 'Who's in here?'

Still no answer, but there was movement: a shadow separated from other shadows. It came from behind a coffin on one of the lowest tiers.

He then heard the deep, menacing growling as the black bulk of the dog slunk from the darkness. Seeker's teeth were bared as it came into the light, and its shoulders were hunched, head low to the ground.

Ash backed away, slowly, cautiously. The dog stalked him, muzzle creased, quivering over pointed teeth that glistened wetly. It snarled throatily, bunching its muscles, hindquarters tensing against the earth floor. It sprang forward.

F I F T E E N

Ash pulled the gate shut, the dog's charge adding impetus from the other side against resisting hinges. He fell away as Seeker's hurled body rocked the bars. The animal became frenzied by its sudden imprisonment, howling at the man lying beyond its reach, yelping in frustration. Slaver from its jaws soaked struts of the rusted gate.

The investigator picked himself up, his eyes never leaving the maddened beast whose ululations were amplified by the stone surroundings. Ash hurried away from the mausoleum, stumbling backwards, body half-crouched as if preparing for the attack should the dog burst through the iron bars. Not until he had reached the edge of the clearing did he turn his back on the dog and run. The sounds of metal clanging against stone and Seeker's frantic barking followed him through the woods. He pushed into foliage, leaping over low obstacles, brushing aside leafy branches that tried to hinder him, not knowing how long the animal could be contained by the unlocked barrier, desperate to put as much distance as possible between him and it.

Voices. No, there couldn't be voices. But there *were*. Around him. In the woods.

He, himself, shouted something, but he had no idea what.

Snickering. God, they were laughing at him. Shadows moving between the trees.

'*Stop this!*' he shouted (or did he scream this time?).

They whispered in return.

Then the crashing of leaves and bushes behind him, as if someone were following, someone or something moving fast. Charging. The dog charging through the undergrowth.

'*Help me!*' he cried out, but their laughter taunted him.

He dare not look, he dare not peek over his shoulder. He might trip, he might fall, he might *see* the black fury bounding after him. The crashing was drawing closer, he was sure he could hear the dog's laboured panting, the rumbled growls as it gained on him; he was certain he could *feel* its hot breath.

His legs felt awkward, as though the knee-joints had loosened, his stride having no rhythm, no coordination. He staggered, each step jolting his body, his lungs seeming to jar against his rib-cage. The dog was almost upon him, he could hear, *he could hear*, the widening of its jaws, the clicking of its teeth, the slopping of its distended tongue . . .

The stark blueness of the sky dazzled him as hands grabbed his chest, a figure blocking his way. He would have collapsed had not those same hands steadied him.

He blinked to clear the mist over his vision (caused by the sudden brightness, or fear's teardrops?).

Standing before him on the open path, so close he could smell the powder on her lined face, and still gripping him tightly, was Nanny Tess. The flowers she had been carrying lay scattered on the ground.

He was too breathless to speak. He could only point back at the woods, his arm wavering, his awkward legs tensed to run.

But there was nothing following him. He could hear the twittering complaints of the birds, his hurtling progress having startled them, and he could see that the foliage and undergrowth were now undisturbed, save for the occasional breeze that ruffled through.

SIXTEEN

Ash rested his elbows on the rough wood of the kitchen table, the cigarette he smoked trembling between his lips. Autumn flowers, those he had knocked from Nanny Tess' arms when he had rushed out onto the woodland path, lay nearby, their petals beginning to lose lustre, but their scent still strong. He inhaled deeply, then took the cigarette from his mouth; now it trembled between his fingers.

Nanny Tess glanced back at him as she poured brandy into a tumbler on the dresser, her face creased with concern. There was the slightest tremor in her own hands. She set down the bottle and, still gripping its neck, she closed her eyes briefly. Then, with resolve, she brought the glass to the table.

'Drink this,' she urged. 'It'll help calm you.'

Ash took a large swallow of the brandy, and another as the Mariells' aunt pulled out a chair to sit at right-angles to him. He felt her scrutiny.

'You say that Seeker went for you again?' she said anxiously. 'He chased after you?'

He nodded and stared into the drink held in both hands on the table top.

114

'But there was no sign of him,' she insisted. 'If Seeker was after you, what made him stop?'

'I don't know.' His voice was low, husky from the brandy. 'Maybe he hid because he saw you. All I know is that he went for me inside . . . inside that bloody tomb.'

She visibly flinched. 'Mr Ash, what made you go to the family grave?'

'Christ, I didn't go there intentionally. I got lost and stumbled into it. Why didn't someone tell me the Mariells had their own mausoleum?'

'It didn't seem important,' she answered. 'Nor is it. I visit once a week to replace flowers, but I'm afraid the place has become terribly neglected, like many other things at Edbrook.' For a moment it was as though her thoughts were elsewhere, in another time.

Ash sipped the brandy, then cleared his throat. 'Christina's parents are buried . . . entombed there?'

'Their remains were brought back from France and laid to rest at Edbrook. You said you found Seeker inside the mausoleum.'

'Yes, skulking somewhere at the back. I thought . . .' he hesitated, shaking his head '. . . I thought Christina was hiding from me in there. She'd left me in the woods, a silly game . . .'

'You must forgive her, Mr Ash – her and her brothers – for their childishness. I believed that the years, all that has happened, would make them change. After their parents' death, I thought grief would help mature them.' Her shoulders slumped, her body seeming to shrink. 'Somehow that tragedy had the opposite effect, as though their loss made the children retreat even more into their world of games and trickery.'

He became impatient. 'Look, the dog – that animal's too bloody dangerous to be running around loose.'

She straightened, became sharp. 'Oh no, Seeker is harmless, Mr Ash. I promise he wouldn't have hurt you. He imagined he was protecting his mistress – he was only trying to frighten you away.'

'What the hell are you talking about? Christina was nowhere around.'

Nanny Tess was saddened rather than taken aback by his anger. 'I had no idea Seeker still guarded her resting place.'

His words were controlled. 'I'm trying to make some sense out of this, Miss Webb, but you're not helping me. Whose resting place?'

She refused to look at him. Her hands fumbled in her lap, strands of white hair hung over her forehead.

'Christina . . .' she began, but faltered. One hand brushed at the wisps of hair. 'Christina had a twin.'

The cigarette stopped before it touched his lips.

'They were so alike,' Nanny Tess went on, 'so very much the same, and yet . . .' She noticed his intense gaze. 'Yes, a sister, Mr Ash, but there was one frightening difference between them.'

He waited, cigarette still poised.

'The other one was a schizophrenic, a normal child one moment, an insane thing the next.'

His question was quietly put. 'She's dead?'

'You saw where she rests, with her mother and father.'

'Something else nobody thought important enough to mention.' He drew fiercely on the cigarette, and expelled smoke in an untidy cloud.

'Why should it mean anything to you?'

'You really don't see? My God, the spectre of a young girl manifests itself in your house and none of you considered the fact that Robert, Simon and Christina had a dead sister relevant? Even when I asked earlier today?'

'It isn't something we like to talk about.'

'Carrying on the family tradition, right?' he retorted disgustedly. 'Well if you want to help this investigation – to help *yourselves*, for God's sake – then you'd better talk about it now.'

Nanny Tess rose from the table, her chair scraping noisily against the tiled floor. She went to the dresser and took another tumbler from the cupboard beneath. This time she poured herself a stiff measure of brandy.

Ash held his own glass up, its contents almost gone. She returned with the bottle and placed it in front of him. He helped himself as she took her seat again.

Nanny Tess drank, grimacing at the taste, before saying, 'I'm not sure . . .'

'You *have* to tell me,' he insisted.

'It was so long ago. I've tried to shut what happened from my mind.'

His tone softened. 'I want you to understand something. If you – if all of you – have been suppressing some dark memory, a terrible event from the past, then it might just be that your collective subconscious – believe me, this can happen – is now pushing that memory to the fore, refusing to allow the girl to be forgotten. Your minds could be working together to bring into being an image – a spirit as far as you're concerned – of Christina's sister. Do you understand what I'm saying?'

Her thoughts were deep. 'I . . . I think so. But you don't believe in the supernatural.'

'No, but I believe in the paranormal. There's a difference. Now will you tell me?'

She raised the tumbler, sipped, took a longer drink. She looked directly at him, as if making up her mind. Then she began to speak.

'My sister and her husband would never admit to the outside world that a child of theirs could be . . . wasn't quite right. You had to know them, Mr Ash, had to know the times they lived in, the attitudes –'

He interrupted. 'The Mariell attitude?'

'There was never any question of sending their daughter away, not to an institution. Not *just* because of the shame, but because of the love they had for their child as well. It's strange now to think of how many times my sister, Isobel, begged me to take care of all her children should anything ever happen to her and her husband. It was almost as if she had a premonition. Is that possible, Mr Ash? Do you think somehow she knew they would both die so very young?'

'Some of my colleagues would say such premonitions are common,' he replied.

She bowed her head, absorbing his response. 'Their terrible deaths shocked us all, but for her, for Christina's sister, the shock must have been the worst. Her poor little mind just couldn't cope with the loss, you see; the bad part of her began to dominate the healthy part more and more. She played the same games as the others, but hers increasingly became more dangerous. They grew afraid of her; eventually they began to resent her. When those black, those foul, moods were upon her, she felt Seeker was her only friend. Her practical jokes became more malicious, so much so that we often had to lock her away, for her own safety as much as the other children's.'

The aunt drank more brandy, as if to steady herself. Ash stubbed out the cigarette in a saucer she had provided. He waited for her to continue.

'Then one night, she somehow managed to set fire to the house – we don't know if it was accidentally or not. We were soon aware of what she had done and managed to put out the fire; but she had disappeared. We searched the house from top to bottom. Only when Simon discovered the back door was open did we realize what had happened. We found her body in the pond.'

Horrified, Ash stared at the Mariells' aunt. Her thoughts were elsewhere, remembering the night.

'Her nightdress had caught fire and she'd thrown herself into the water to douse the flames, you see. But her injuries must have been too severe, she must have been too weak to drag herself out. She drowned, Mr Ash, the poor child drowned.'

He was stunned, barely able to think clearly. 'Yesterday morning, when Christina was showing me the grounds, she seemed afraid to go near the pond . . .'

'None of us like being near it, even after all this time. That's why the pond has become so neglected.'

Ash sat back in the chair, confused, giving himself time to allow what she had said to sink in. 'I still don't understand why you haven't told me this before,' he said.

'Why should we speak of madness within our family? We've always protected each other, even our memories. It wasn't for you to know, Mr Ash. Until now, that is. Now I feel you have the right.'

'And is there more that you should tell me?'

She gave a slow shake of her head. 'There are matters here at Edbrook that should never be delved into by outsiders.'

Nanny Tess drained the rest of her brandy, then got up from the table.

'Wait . . .' Ash said urgently as she walked away.

She opened the kitchen door and turned. 'My advice to you,' she said, 'is to leave this house. No good will come of your investigation. Can't *you* feel that, too?'

Nanny Tess left the room.

S E V E N T E E N

Cigarette smoke poisoned the air, curling in the shafts of light from the bedroom window. Ash read through his notes, his face grimly angry, then laid the felt-tip down. He stubbed out the last half-inch of the cigarette into a brass ashtray. He reached for the vodka bottle, whose level was now well below the halfway mark, and was stopped from drinking by a sharp knock on the door.

Simon Mariell looked in, not bothering to wait for a reply. 'Have you got a few minutes?' he asked, wearing the supercilious grin that was beginning to irritate Ash more each time he saw it. 'Robert would like to see you in the drawing room.'

Ash bit on his anger. 'Yeah, and I think I'd like to see him.'

He pulled on his jacket, which had been draped over the back of his chair and went to the door. Simon was already some way down the corridor and Ash followed, disliking the sunless gloom in that part of the house, the smell of dust and old wood particularly unpleasant there.

He descended the wide staircase, tired from the brandy so early in the day, the nips of vodka afterwards in his room. He noticed for the first time how worn the stair carpet was at its edges.

In the drawing room, Robert, Christina and Nanny Tess

were waiting for him. Simon closed the door behind Ash, then took a seat next to Christina on a long sofa.

Robert, who had been standing by one of the spacious room's deep windows, came forward, his smile cool. 'I wondered if we might have some sort of progress report, Mr Ash,' he said.

'Just what stupid kind of game d'you think you're playing?' replied the investigator.

Christina jerked in her seat, startled by his response.

But Robert's tone was mild, and his smile remained. 'I'm not sure I understand . . .'

'The incident last night. And today, Christina leading me to the family mausoleum where that bloody dog was waiting for me again.'

'But I didn't –' Christina protested.

He rounded on her. 'You just happened to run off in that direction, is that it? And the voices I heard in the woods – they were only in my imagination?' He faced Robert once more. 'A little while ago, your aunt told me a cock and bull story about another sister of yours, Christina's twin, who drowned here at Edbrook years ago.' He shot an angry look at Nanny Tess, who was perched on the edge of an armchair, her frail body rigid. 'She almost had me convinced. It fits in so snugly with the haunting you've asked me to investigate, doesn't it?'

'I'm afraid your recent experiences have made you somewhat overwrought,' Robert said smoothly. 'Why on earth should we go to such lengths?'

'That's what I'd like *you* to tell me. Is it some nasty little plot you and certain others have hatched to discredit me? Retribution for all the fake hauntings and phoney spiritualists I've exposed over the years? Don't tell me you've all got together in a pathetic attempt to undermine those past investigations.'

Robert's manner remained mild. 'I wonder if you're aware of how ridiculous you're being. Yes, your vendetta against certain psychics and supernatural phenomena is well known;

121

but that's of no interest to the Mariell family. We're not involved in such matters.'

'I only have your word on that. What the hell do I really know about you – any of you?'

Ash glared around at all of them. Christina appeared uncertain, anxious, while Nanny Tess was obviously alarmed at his outburst. Yet Simon was hiding a smirk behind his hand. Which angered the investigator even more.

Robert walked to the empty fireplace and rested a hand on its mantel. 'We've told you everything we thought was necessary. If you feel you need to know more, then we're willing to co-operate in any way we can. However, it seems you even doubt Nanny's word.'

'Only because she spoke of Christina's twin as though she had died many years ago – when she was no more than a child. So how could Seeker have been her special pet?' He brushed a hand through his hair, agitated. 'That's what Miss Webb told me. Even now he guards the girl's resting place, she said. Well I'm no expert on animals, but I don't need to be to see that the dog isn't that old. Her story was just a stupid lie.' He waved at the air, shaking his head. 'And that made me wonder about everything else. The thing I don't understand is what you hoped to gain by discrediting me.'

'We only want the truth, Mr Ash,' the elder Mariell told him. 'Only that.'

Christina rose from the sofa and went to the investigator, who regarded her warily. 'David, perhaps it's your own prejudices that make you doubt us,' she said.

His answer was cold. 'I'd say my prejudices are healthy. Unlike your games.'

'Ah, you really believe this is all a game,' said Robert from across the room. 'Then go ahead, prove it's so. Or, if you can't do that, prove that the disturbances in this house – and remember, you've experienced some unnatural moments here yourself – prove that they're caused by subterranean springs, hidden faults in Edbrook's structure, or so-called electromagnetic impulses. Prove the "phenomena" are natural, or prove they're trickery. You might even show us we're mistaken in our belief that our home is haunted. We'd all be very interested in your rationalizations, Mr Ash. And, of course, I'm sure the Psychical Research Institute would be also.'

'Why the hell should I bother?'

Simon chuckled. 'Because of your own professional curiosity. Why else?'

'Oh, and I think more than that,' his brother added. 'You need your personal belief, Mr Ash, and that's in your own scepticism. Nevertheless, as a more material reason, I'm willing to treble your normal fee for such an investigation, as well as make a substantial donation towards your Institute's general researches. The latter counts only if you prove conclusively that there really is no ghost at Edbrook.' He spread his hands in a placatory gesture. 'Is it a challenge you're prepared to accept?'

Ash searched each face before giving his answer. 'Okay,' he said slowly. 'Okay, but I want a promise that tonight, no matter what happens here, none of you will leave your rooms. It's the only way I can be sure you won't be involved in any disturbances.'

Robert smiled his assurance. 'Simon and I will be spending the night in London – we have an early business meeting in the City tomorrow morning – so at least you won't have to worry about us playing tricks on you. I'm sure Christina and Nanny will agree to your condition.'

The aunt turned away, while Christina looked directly at him and nodded, her former anxiety no longer evident.

'Maybe I'll have the answers on your return,' Ash told Robert.

'I hope so,' the other man replied. 'Yes, I do hope so.'

EIGHTEEN

The figure trudged the country lane, thick woodland on either side screening distant slopes, and although still bright, the air itself was more chilled now that the sun had passed its zenith.

Ash pulled up the lapels of his jacket, wishing he'd taken time to go to his room for his overcoat before leaving Edbrook. His stride was brisk, the exercise and the cold having a revitalizing effect, his earlier tiredness shed completely.

Nevertheless, by the time he reached the telephone box, which stood as though planted on a small triangle of overgrown grass at a junction with a wider road, Ash was out of breath, his legs stiff with the unaccustomed exertion. The box was of the older breed – uncompromising red (yet, perversely, just right in any surroundings), with several panes of glass either missing or cracked – and the investigator hoped it hadn't been forgotten entirely by its overlords. With some effort, he swung the door open and lifted the receiver. Good, it *burred*. Ash laid a selection of coins on the shelf and found what he was looking for. He dialled a number, paused, pushed in the coin.

'Kate McCarrick,' he said.

While he waited for the connection, he looked through one of the small windows back along the lane. His breath misted the glass.

'Kate? It's me, David.'

Her voice sounded concerned. 'David. Why haven't you called before? We've been worried.'

'I couldn't,' he told her. 'The phone at Edbrook is out of action. Permanently so, it seems.'

'There's no telephone listed for Edbrook.'

He frowned, silent for a moment.

'David, did you hear me? I said there's no phone listed for the Mariells.'

There was a weariness to his reply. 'Yeah, I heard. They're a surprising family. Look, d'you know anything about the Mariells, their background?'

At the Psychical Research Institute Kate removed her reading glasses and laid them on the desk. 'Only what was in Miss Webb's two letters, and that was precious little,' she said. 'I could try and check them out for you, but I don't have much time today – I'm preparing for the Parapsychological Conference tomorrow. You know how busy –' she held the receiver away from her ear as a sudden burst of static crackled through the line. 'You still there, David?' she asked when the interference had passed. 'This is an awful line.'

'Do your best for me, Kate,' she heard him say, his voice faint. 'I'm not quite sure what I'm dealing with here. I don't know if they're frauds or genuine.'

She was firm. 'If there's a problem, just drop it. There's no need to get involved.'

Ash wiped away the mist on the window pane with his fingers. His grin was humourless. 'You don't know what they're offering,' he said into the mouthpiece.

There was more distortion on the line, the crackling unpleasantly sharp.

'I didn't catch that,' came Kate's voice. 'What did you say?'

He raised his voice-level to be heard. 'It's not important. I'm going to see it through, Kate. It's an unusual case. Look,

I haven't got any more coins, so I can't talk long. I'll get back to you tomorrow.'

'I'll be at the conference. Tell me more about what's happening there.'

'I wish I knew myself,' he answered. 'But Robert Mariell's laid down an interesting challenge –'

The urgent *pipping* informed him his time had run out.

'I'll call you tomorrow evening, Kate,' he said quickly. 'At home. Tell you more then –'

The line disconnected, *burring* once more.

In her office, Kate glared at the telephone. 'David? Damn!' She replaced the receiver, scowling as she did so. She looked towards Edith Phipps, who was watching her from across the room.

He approached the house through the gardens, leaving the long drive to cut across lawns. Ash stopped to lean against a tree and give his legs a needed rest. You're getting old, he told himself, feeling inside his jacket pocket for the cigarette pack. He observed the building in the distance, its façade faded and aged, less grand than it obviously had been a century ago. One or two of the chimney stacks had chunks of masonry missing from their corners and even from this far away he could see that paintwork around windows was flaked and cracked, that guttering here and there was loose, tiles missing from the roof. The Mariells had allowed the house to deteriorate, and he wondered why. Was their financial position shaky? Apparently not so bad that Robert couldn't afford to pay Ash treble his normal fee, as well as donate a lump sum to the Institute itself. In any case, Ash had investigated similar properties, as well as larger ones, whose upkeep had been somewhat neglected by their gentry owners, and often, unless previous death duties had dwindled the family's wealth, it amounted to nothing more than a peculiar kind of carelessness.

About to light the cigarette, something caught his eye.

Ahead of him, and so still he hadn't noticed, someone else was watching the house. A figure in white.

A cold breeze touched his spine.

It was a girl, dark hair loose around her shoulders.

Ash took the cigarette from his mouth and tucked it into his top pocket. Cautiously he moved towards her, almost as if afraid any noise would make her – would make her *image* – disappear. A foolish notion, he told himself, but still he trod carefully.

As he drew close, he heard her soft, melancholic humming, a tune he had heard once before, although he could not remember when. A simple cadence, like that of a nursery rhyme, and somehow haunting.

A few feet away, and the hair, the narrow shoulders, were familiar.

Close enough to touch.

The tune stopped. Christina turned and smiled up at him.

'I didn't mean to startle you,' he apologized, standing there awkwardly.

'I was waiting for you,' she said.

Ash remembered Christina had hummed that same tune on their way back from the station the day before. He walked around the garden bench and sat beside her.

'Aren't you cold?' he asked. Although the dress was long, reaching almost to her ankles, the sleeves touching her wrists, it was of a light material.

She shrugged. 'You were gone a long time,' she said.

'It's quite a way to the phone box.'

She regarded him quizzically.

'I had to ring the Institute, let them know what's going on,' he explained. 'Easier said than done, considering I'm mystified myself. Why isn't the phone in the house working?'

'Oh, we *hate* telephones. It's so nasty talking to discarnate voices.' She smiled again, that subtle mocking in her eyes.

He ignored it. 'But how d'you get by? How do your brothers conduct their business affairs?'

'We manage somehow.'

She began to hum the tune again, as though uninterested in the conversation.

Ash leaned forward, resting his elbows on his knees. Like her, he looked towards Edbrook. 'Why did you leave me alone in the woods?' he said.

The tune stopped, and she seemed truly regretful when she said, 'I didn't mean to. I thought you were right behind me. Do you forgive me?'

'Wasn't it another one of your games? Something that you and Simon – and probably Robert, too – devised among you? Something to give me a little scare?'

The rhyme again, mournfully intoned in a minor key.

'What business are your brothers in, Christina?' Ash persisted. 'How do they manage the upkeep on a place like Edbrook?'

'I thought I told you. My father left us money. Investments, stocks and shares – I don't get involved. That's why Robert and Simon have gone to London.'

'Yet you don't have enough wealth to pay for staff. It's a big estate for your aunt to run all on her own.'

'She hires people when necessary. In the spring and summer gardeners come in to take care of the grounds. But mostly we like to be alone.'

'Why should that be?'

'Because we have each other. We don't need outsiders.'

He turned to face her. 'Don't you ever feel the need to get away, Christina? Don't you ever leave Edbrook?'

'Oh yes.' She smiled at him. 'Yes, frequently. For long, long periods at a time.'

But now Ash was staring past her at someone standing beneath a group of trees on the far side of the lawns. A diminutive figure, shaded from the sun by overhead branches. A small girl, too far away for him to determine her features or her age. White ankle socks indicated she was very young.

Christina was still talking, unaware his attention was elsewhere. 'I'm always drawn back to Edbrook. I don't think I could ever really leave . . .'

He touched her arm. 'Look, Christina, over there. Can you see her?'

She looked to where he indicated. 'I can't see anyone.'

'There, by the trees.'

She squinted her eyes, peering intently. She shook her head at him. 'I still can't see . . .'

He looked at her in surprise. 'Surely . . .' Ash gently guided her face with his hand.

But now there was no one there. No figure stood beneath the trees.

NINETEEN

He wandered through the house, its emptiness an oppressive thing, his footsteps loud, echoing in the hallways. Ash was not completely alone, for Christina and her aunt were in their rooms, yet his sense of isolation was difficult to shrug off. Outside, the night was clear, cloudless, the moon proud and crisp in its uncontested rule; the building's old walls seemed to be absorbing the atmosphere's coldness rather than fending it off, for everything, even furniture, felt frigid to the touch.

He had dined alone that evening, Nanny Tess barely speaking when she had set the meal before him. But then Ash, himself, had been in no mood for conversation. When he had enquired after Christina, assuming that her brothers had already departed for London, he was informed by Nanny Tess that her niece had retired early, the late activities of the previous night no doubt having their effect. The aunt had added that last remark as though it was *his* fault.

In various rooms he checked the detection equipment, ensuring that each piece would function properly should anything trigger it off. He sprinkled more powder, finding new locations to layer, then made sure all outside doors were closed and locked. Floorboards creaked beneath his feet as he went from room to room, and where his fingers brushed against walls and banisters, he noticed they came away smeared with dust. Something else he noticed, and which he hadn't before, were the cobwebs: they hung in dark corners like tattered miniature drapes, matted with dirt, the worst of them in the furthest reaches of the house in rooms that obviously were rarely used. He shook his head in disgust. The Mariells expected too much of their aunt if they imagined she could take care of the property all on her own. No wonder she appeared so agitated.

In one room a spider scuttled across his hand as he reached in and flicked on the light switch. Ash flinched, his flesh crawling at the tickling sensation. He watched the spider disappear into a hole in the skirting board. The light was dim, as it was throughout Edbrook, and he wondered why he hadn't come upon this particular room before. Then he remembered it had previously been locked and, as the Mariells had alleged no 'sightings' inside, he had left it alone. Perhaps they had now left it open so that he could have full run of the house.

The furniture was covered in dust sheets and, above the mantel opposite, was a portrait of a man and a woman, both of them in formal evening dress. He had the eerie feeling of being under their inspection.

There was no doubting who the subjects were, for the woman bore an undeniable resemblance to Christina, although this woman's countenance was less soft, her hair lighter in shade, dissimilar in style; but the eyes were the same, their hidden amusement skilfully captured by the artist, enigmatic in that they were not quite mocking, nor were they warm. They seemed to express an inner knowledge.

The man was altogether more austere, an older, more rigid, version of Robert. If there was humour in this person's life, it had been kept well at bay at the time of the sitting. The stern features offered scant insight into the nature of the man.

Thomas and Isobel Mariell, deceased parents of Robert, Simon and Christina. Isobel, sister of Tessa Webb.

Their unflinching gaze made Ash uncomfortable. He turned off the light and closed the door.

As he walked back along the hallway, he was aware of the vapour of his own breath. He checked the nearest thermometer and found the reading very low. Nine degrees C. How cold did it have to get before the family switched on Edbrook's antiquated heating system, or at least lit fires in the many hearths around their home?

He reached the library, entered. And was blinded by white light.

Ash cursed as his hands went to his stinging eyes, realizing he must have left on the capacitance change detector. A white sheet of film whirred from the Polaroid camera and dropped to the floor. The spools of the small tape recorder slowly revolved. Blinking his eyes rapidly and shielding them from another flash, he made his way towards the tripod-mounted camera. Another blank sheet emerged and landed by the previous one. Light flared again.

He fumbled for the button on the detector and discovered it was already off. Impossible! The machine couldn't operate in that mode. He yanked out the connecting wire to the camera.

The flash once more, like sheet lightning. The whir of expelled film. The tape spools still turning.

'Impossible!' This time he said it aloud.

Blinding brightness yet again. In incredible succession. Film was spewing from the camera's mouth. And he could hear the tapes as they spun faster.

Ash stumbled towards the plug socket, tripping over furniture as he went, unable to see for more than a second at a time. He crouched, reaching down, ready to pull the plug by its flex.

The flashes ceased. The last developing print fell from the camera. Tape snaked into a looping arc as the spools stopped dead. There was no sound in the room other than his own breathing.

Ash was stunned. It was inconceivable that the instrument

should malfunction in such a way, that the camera, once disconnected, should operate on its own. Had there been some kind of power surge, enough to upset the delicate mechanism of the capacitance change detector? He glanced up at the dull light. He had noticed nothing as he'd entered the room, but perhaps the surge had happened just as the door opened, the camera flash instantly spoiling his vision. Yet the detector hadn't been switched on. Had that mattered? Ash rose from his crouched position, baffled, but suspecting trickery of some sort.

He went to the scattered prints on which images were emerging like shapes from a mist. Bending down, he picked up two whose development was more advanced than the others; he examined them closely. One showed his figure in the doorway; in the other he was approaching the camera itself. He squatted to sift through the rest on the floor. The colours and shapes surfaced steadily so that he could see his own image growing larger in each shot, then smaller as he retreated towards the wall socket. Apart from the surrounds, that was all that the prints revealed.

Ash shuffled the photographs into a neat pile and slipped them into his jacket pocket. He left the library, confused, but without touching the equipment again. Closing the door behind him, he paused for a moment in the hallway and listened.

There were voices coming from somewhere. Hushed voices, little more than whispers.

'Christina?' he said loudly. 'Miss Webb?'

Silence now.

He went to other doors, looked in, searching. They were all empty.

Ash climbed the stairs, taking the opposite direction to his own room when he reached the corridor. He stopped outside Christina's bedroom and knocked softly. There was no response. He called her name, but still no reply came.

He went further along to mount a narrow set of stairs that twisted round to the floor above. In the distant past, the rooms up there must have been occupied by Edbrook's servants, but he knew that this was now where the Mariells' aunt had her living quarters. There were several doors along the rough-boarded corridor, and he tapped on each one. Again, he received no answer.

He stood there for a while, in that shadowy place, mystified. Apart from himself, the house appeared to be empty.

When he returned to the ground floor, his face was resolute. The Mariells were playing another of their stupid games, setting him up, trying to unnerve him, obviously an attempt to render his imagination more susceptible to . . . to what? What could be their purpose? Did they really believe they could frighten him again? Did they expect him to flee from the house, scared away by the inexplicable? To become a figure of scorn to others in his profession? He smiled grimly. It would take more than this family's fun and games to do that.

On the last step he came to a halt. He listened intently.

One voice this time.

A tune being hummed.

That same melancholic tune he had heard from Christina earlier that day.

Ash took the last step into the hall and walked to its centre where he slowly turned a full circle in an attempt to get a bearing on the sound.

The cellar door was ajar. The voice drifted up from its depths.

Although his footsteps were soft as he approached the open doorway, the faint humming stopped.

He bent close to the gap, waiting, listening, a draught chilling his face. Nothing.

Ash pushed the door further open and felt inside for the light switch he knew was at the top of the cellar stairs. The light was poorer than before, casting even deeper shadows.

He descended, the wooden steps groaning under his weight.

Once at the bottom, he took in the broad, rough-bricked chamber, alcoves on one side dark and impenetrable, cobwebs clinging untidily from low rafters, covered furniture and broken statues scattered here and there. The smell of dankness and mould seemed stronger.

'Christina, are you down here?' His voice was controlled. It sounded hollow within the confines of the basement. Only silence greeted him.

It was difficult to restrain his anger. 'If this is another silly bloody game . . .'

Somehow the silence was mocking.

He shivered, feeling the bitter cold. The thermometer hanging from a rack registered three degrees C. A quiet click made him turn. The camera's motor wound the film on, Ash's presence having been recorded. The shutter clicked again at his approach and he quickly switched it off. He noticed the tape recorder, positioned on a shelf along with a vibration detector, was running, and Ash wondered if he had set it in motion, or had someone else before him? He pressed REWIND.

As he waited, he lit a cigarette, the inhaled smoke a small comfort against the icy atmosphere. The tape reversed to a stop and he touched the PLAY button. For a second or two there was only a barely audible hissing, then he stiffened when he heard footsteps from the machine.

They grew louder, descending the steps. A pause. Ash wasn't quite sure if he was relieved or disappointed to hear his own voice say: 'Christina, are you down here?'

He pressed STOP and switched off the machine at its power source. Resting back against a wine rack, Ash drew deeply on the cigarette, the question returning: Why? What the hell were they up to? What did they expect to achieve? He scanned the cellar until he was reasonably satisfied there was no one else down there with him, glad he had insisted that the dog be shut outside the house for the night. Christina's voice? Either he'd been mistaken, or there were pipes or a shaft that might have carried the sound to the basement from elsewhere in the building. That had to be the explanation, surely. He still had no idea how they'd managed to override the power switch for the equipment in the library, but somehow they had. Tomorrow he would find out, even if it meant taking the machinery apart, piece by piece.

His throat felt dry and he had to admit to himself, despite his rationalizations, his nerves were unsettled. Idiot! He was allowing the Mariells to get to him. Angry, he pulled a wine bottle from the rack and wiped dust from the label with the palm of his hand. Château Cheval-Blanc, 1932. No doubt a good year. He pushed it back and reached for another. More vintage wine, he realized with some envy. Château Climens, 1929. Ash moved further along to find shelf spaces among the racks, inside these alcohol of a harder nature. He took down an Armagnac and peeled at the neck wax with a thumbnail. Let the Mariells complain, he grumbled to himself. Maybe I'll just counter-complain. Cigarette dangling between his lips, he twisted off the bottle's top.

A muffled giggle came from somewhere in the cellar.

He turned sharply, in time to catch a shadow move inside one of the alcoves. In his surprise, the brandy slipped from his grasp, the cigarette fell from his mouth. The glass shattered against the stone, its contents exploding outwards, splattering Ash's trousers, spreading across the floor in a shiny pool.

Ash's startled cry rang round the cellar when the alcohol burst into flame.

Shocked, he leapt backwards. He saw there were flaming patches on his trousers and hastily slapped them out, moving further away from the fire as he did so.

Grabbing a dustsheet, he ran forward again and threw it over the flames, smothering them completely. He stamped on the covering, crunching broken glass beneath, working systematically so that the whole area was covered, fearful that the material itself would catch alight.

He had no time to consider the sly noise that had caused the freak accident, but realized that the cigarette he had dropped must have ignited the brandy; he was now concerned only with snuffing the fire before it had a chance to take hold.

Moments later he sagged against the wine rack, the battle won, the sheet blackened and charred. The shock and the exertion had drenched his body in perspiration. He felt hot. He felt as if he were burning up.

Cautiously he lifted the smouldering dustsheet. The fire was out, with not even a scorchmark on the stone. Yet when he straightened, he saw orange reflections dancing on the walls and ceiling of the underground chamber.

He looked around, wildly. It couldn't be! The fire was out! But flickering shadows stated otherwise.

His legs were burning. He stepped back, slapping at them once more. But there was no fire. There was no fire, yet he could *feel* the heat of it! And it was becoming difficult to breathe as oxygen was absorbed. And he could *hear* the fire's crackle.

But there was no fire!

As if to reassure his sensibilities, as if to reason with himself, he checked the thermometer. To his dismay, the mercury was rising rapidly. It was soaring. So fast, so unbelievably fast!

Ash felt weak, the heat sapping his strength. Breathing had become torturous.

He fell away as the thermometer glass shattered, hands instinctively protecting his face from the shards.

Its explosive violence galvanized Ash into action. He staggered towards the stairs, clawing at his shirt collar as he went, choking on unseen smoke. He stumbled blindly against the wooden steps, feeling their brittle heat as he pushed himself upwards, desperate to get out of the cellar. Flames and moving shadows flickered on the walls around him. He could hear the *crumple* of burning wood. Soon the bottles would burst from the heat, their discharge encouraging the fire, feeding it. He could feel – could smell – his clothes smouldering, could feel the tightening of his skull as his hair stiffened, became dry.

Ash forced himself to climb, gasping for air, the heat searing his skin. He was near the top. The cellar door was closed.

He stretched a hand towards the handle, yelling when his fingers closed on the hot metal.

He collapsed onto his knees, holding his burnt hand with the other. His breathing was painful, his senses were swimming from the lack of pure air. Ash pulled a handkerchief from his pocket and used it to grasp the metal again.

His hand slipped.

Below him, the inferno raged. He cringed against its roar.

This time he used both hands over bundled handkerchief, ignoring the pain, forcing the handle to turn.

The lock released. He pulled the door inwards. And his eyes grew bright with new horror.

Looming over him was the darkened figure of a girl, her hair wild around her face, her nightgown flowing outwards as though tossed by the storm below.

T W E N T Y

The figure leaned towards him, a blackened shape whose
features for the moment remained unseen. Ash cringed
inwards, his muscles tightening, shrinking from her touch.

But as she drew near, her face lightened as if revealed by
the invisible flames, and it was Christina's concerned eyes
that searched his, Christina's gentle hand that lit upon his
shoulder. Her lips formed his name, though he did not hear.
He saw the fiery flickers reflected in her pupils, flames that
quickly diminished as the heat at his back cooled and the
rumbling sounds of burning died.

A movement behind her caught his eye. Seeker accompanied Christina, but stayed back, head low, shoulders
quivering, looking balefully towards the cellar steps. The
mewled whimpers from its squeezed throat were almost
childlike in their misery.

Ash found that he could only rise with the girl's help, such
was the extent of his shock. She tugged beneath his arms,
lifting, and he had to cling to the doorframe for leverage.

He leaned against her and she sagged under his weight.
When he turned to scream at the inferno below there were
no flames and there was no heat.

The wooden steps merely led down to a cold, dank cellar

where the dim light bulb swayed, sending shadows rushing from one wall to the other.

Edith awoke, the nightmare still parading through her mind. She sprang up in bed, her panic related to the panic in her dream.

Her throat was hoarse as she sucked in air as though the smoke from the nightmare was in her own bedroom. Her breasts heaved, the effort of breathing laboured, her windpipe shrunken against the imaginary fumes; but the pain it caused shifted, clutching at her chest.

Edith knew the signs, knew this searing was not part of the dream, but was real and familiar. She struggled to reach the bedside lamp, panic barely contained, blinking away tears that had as much to do with fright as the hurting. Plump fingers felt the switch. Light shone down on the pill bottle that stood near the lamp's base. The top was hurriedly loosened, a glyceryl trinitrate tablet shaken into the palm of a hand. Edith pushed it beneath her tongue and rested back against the pillow, waiting for the tablet to dissolve and subdue the pain demon, aware that on this occasion the beast might refuse to be caged. But the agony gradually softened and her breathing eventually eased. Her shaking subsided to a trembling.

Sometimes Edith would spit out the glyceryl trinitrate tablet before it had dissolved completely, for the headache it could bring on was almost as fearsome as the torment in her chest. This night she did not.

Supported by the girl, Ash lurched through the bedroom door, a man drunk not from alcohol but from shock and fatigue. His body flagged with the very toil of breathing.

Christina laid him on the bed, lifting his legs so that he was supine. She left him, going to the bureau where she poured vodka into a tumbler.

'The fire . . .' he murmured when she returned.

Christina took his hand and placed the drink in it. 'There was no fire, David. Don't you understand that? It's just part of the haunting.'

He rested on an elbow and said nothing more until he had taken a large gulp of vodka. He winced at its sting, then looked at her, shaking his head. 'That's not possible. The heat –'

'It was in your mind,' Christina insisted gently. 'There wasn't a fire in the cellar, only a memory.'

Thoughts tussled inside his head. 'Your sister . . . it was true, you did have a twin. She started the fire in the cellar all those years ago.'

Christina looked down on him as if in pity. 'There's no danger, David. You're perfectly safe.'

'She was burned down there . . .'

'You're shivering. Let me cover you.'

Christina helped him out of his jacket, then removed his shoes. She pulled the blanket over him and sat down on the edge of the bed, her hand smoothing dark hair away from his forehead. Her fingers lingered on his cheek.

His breathing not yet settled, Ash looked pleadingly at her. 'Christina, tell me what's happening here at Edbrook.'

Her reply was not meant to be unkind. 'Weren't you going to tell us that?' Her hand slid to his shoulder. 'Just rest, David, push all those bad thoughts from your mind. You look so pale, so tired.'

But he persisted. 'Yesterday . . . a few minutes after I arrived . . . I thought I saw you in the garden with Simon. But it couldn't have been you . . .'

'Try to calm yourself.'

'There's another girl here . . .'

'We've tried to tell you that. Rest, David.'

His exhaustion was not easily resisted. He grabbed her wrist. 'I came to your room earlier – you weren't there.'

He found her voice soothing despite his agitation. 'I've kept to my room since early evening, just as you requested. I must have been sleeping when you knocked – I sleep very soundly, David.'

'But Miss Webb – she didn't answer either when I went to her room.'

Christina smiled reassuringly, as might a mother whose child was afraid of the red-eyed monster lurking in the bedroom closet. 'Nanny often takes sleeping pills at night – she hasn't slept well for years. I doubt you'd have roused her even if you'd beaten down the door.' She dabbed abstractedly at the edge of the blanket, smoothing its rumpled line. 'Perhaps you did disturb my sleep – I don't know. I seem to remember having a bad dream, a nightmare. I woke sensing something was wrong. I couldn't obey your instructions, David, I had to leave my room and find out what was troubling me.'

'I'm glad you did,' he told her. He sighed wearily, realizing how exhausted he was. His eyes closed for a moment, glass resting against his chest. Christina took it from him to place it on the bedside cabinet.

His eyes opened again. 'Tell me about your sister . . .'

She glanced away, giving a small shake of her head as if such memories were too distressing. A tear slowly glistened a path on her pale cheek. Ash gently coaxed her down beside him.

'I know, Christina,' he whispered, 'I know how it hurts. I miss my own sister, even though it was so long ago when she . . . she . . .'

Christina raised her head so that she could search his eyes. 'Why is it so difficult for you to say? She drowned, and for some reason you can't accept the word. Why does it make you so afraid, David?'

His reply was cold, toneless, a dull acceptance. 'Because it was my fault.' Disbelief, confusion – whatever her expression might have been, he repeated his guilt. 'It was my fault that she drowned.'

He stared beyond Christina, looking into a distance of which time was the measurement. And the memories came easily, those childhood times that had been held at bay for so many years, contained like some terrible blight that might cause havoc if allowed freedom. They now emerged as if from a broken chrysalis of consciousness. He wondered, himself, at the outflow, dismayed that they could so suddenly pour through unchecked, arriving to taunt him, to remind him of events past that would best be forgotten. But nothing is truly lost from the mind's labyrinthal vaults: although traumas may be hidden, perhaps placated, not all can be laid to rest; some merely lie low in anticipation of future arousal. Yet strangely, they brought with them a peculiar relief. Ash talked, and as he did so, visions played before him, their retrieval a smooth and unstoppable dredging. Ash shuddered inwardly as he remembered.

'Juliet was a spiteful kid. Even after all these years I can remember her for that. To tell you the truth, I've no fond memories of her at all. Isn't that a terrible thing to admit, Christina? My own sister, killed when she was only a kid, and I can't find anything good to say about her, even though I miss her so much. She was a couple of years older than me, you see, and her great delight was to tease, to make me suffer. I honestly believe she resented sharing our parents' love with me. But her pranks went beyond just sibling jealousy . . .'

He was watching himself as a boy.

'. . . There was always something cruel in her teasing, her tricks . . .'

. . . The little boy's face crumples to tears as his sister snaps off the wing of his model aeroplane, her smile pleasant enough, but a gleaming in her eyes that bids only contempt . . .

. . . A small foot, slyly protruding from beneath a table, tripping the boy as he passes by laden with dinner plates . . .

. . . The boy, a little older now, nudged in his sleep, awakened by a stiffened claw scraping his cheek. David screams and his sister scurries back to her own bed as footsteps are heard

143

along the corridor, the dismembered claw quickly hidden beneath the blankets . . .

And Ash was absorbed into his younger self; he saw what he once saw . . .

. . . Excitedly, breath held, he watches the pale form of the fish approaching the fishing line, its movements jerky and cautious, resisting the river's swift current with delicate twists. The fish nibbles at the bait and David's grip on the crude rod tightens. But he utters a shout of dismay as a clod of earth shatters the water's surface and the fish darts away in rapid angular sprints.

David whirls to find Juliet laughing at him, and he yells his outrage, which only increases her taunting. He lays the short home-made fishing rod on the footpath and runs at his sister, fists clenched as puny weapons; but Juliet easily dodges his rush and scoops up the rod. She teases him with it, poking his stomach, swishing it dangerously in the air, forcing him to keep his distance.

David cries out as the stick catches his cheek, drawing a thin line of blood.

He touches the wound, then studies the red slicks left on his fingertips.

The girl backs away from him, no fear in her step for she still laughs, mocking him, deriding the cut to his flesh. She moves close to the riverbank and, with a contemptuous sneer spoiling her pretty features, turns and calmly throws the fishing rod into the river. The stick of bamboo quickly hurries away, drawn into the stronger currents at the river's centre.

It is more than this one cool and wicked gesture that incenses the boy, for his sister's spite is no fresh thing: years of such artful and pernicious abuse have moulded a fury which has always before seemed to congeal inside his chest; now it is loosened, decongested, made free to rise as a gusher of hate. He tears towards his sister, hands clawed to grasp her.

As her tormenting had aroused his anger, so his anger at last arouses her fear. She stumbles away, avoiding his reach.

David sees the danger, his hands tensing in a different way, this time to restrain her.

But she mistakes his intention – or perhaps she loathes him too much to allow his touch. Another faltering step backwards. And she falls.

His hand has the material of her dress and he is pulled with her, his own momentum pitching him forward. They descend as one, brother and sister, irrevocably tied. Into the river.

Cold, cold embrace. A blurred cosmos of ponderous, muffled sounds and shadows. A breath-stealing place of infinite greyness.

The boy rises, although his will has nothing to do with the feat: the rushing currents merely toss him upwards like flotsam. He spins, head above the surface, and catches a brief sight of his father running towards the riverbank, his mother close behind, the picnic flask forgetfully clutched in her hand. Their mouths are wide with unheard cries.

David is dragged down again as if by invisible hands and his eyes close against the stinging weight that probes them. He knows he must not scream, for his throat and then his lungs will be clogged with the greyness; yet it's impossible not to.

Hands that are more substantial now take hold, his father in the turmoiled water with him. He is pulled away from the other tenacious grip, a rag doll torn between opposing claimants – the avaricious current and the possessive patriarch. It is the man who gradually begins to win the prize.

David rises above the running surface once more and this time he glimpses the darkly matted hair of his sister, not yet far away, but swiftly becoming so.

She disappears, sucked down as if swallowed, a tiny waving hand the last to be seen of her.

David is dumped roughly against the riverbank, his mother's hands, the flask finally dropped from them, dragging his wet and frail body upwards. His father plunges back into the deeper parts of the river, his desperate haste shattering the water's surface. He dives, his feet momentarily kicking air, and the woman and boy, huddled together on the footpath, watch wretch-edly.

After what seems an interminable time, David's father rises, jaws open to gulp air. He dives again.

And to the boy the world is suddenly silent, a doleful void without sound and time, though movement is present, for the river still races, the grass still bends to the breeze. A neverness of waiting, an infinite lull.

Broken by the father's despairing wail as he explodes from the water once again, his daughter lost in the weighty gloom below.

David jerks, startled by the terrible anguish in his father's cry; his mother's grip tightens around him, clutching as if to hold him where he will forever be safe.

He cowers against her breast, one eye staring out at his sister's abductor. There comes a blankness to that vision as his father's wailing grows louder, the rushing of the water swells to a thunderous roar . . .

. . . His head against the pillow, close to Christina's, Ash's vision was as blank as the boy's all those years ago on the riverbank. And the numbing hurt was no less acute.

'I never told them,' he said, voice dull. 'I never told anyone it was my fault, that I'd pushed Juliet into the river.'

'But it was an accident,' Christina said.

'No. I meant her to drown. In that one insane moment I wanted her to die. I know I tried to help her, but . . . but when my father came out of that river, I was relieved, some dark part of me was glad.' The admission, after years of confused and unconvincing denial to himself, staggered him. 'I'm not sure which feeling of guilt has been worse since that day – guilt because of what I'd done, or what I felt afterwards.'

'You've tortured yourself all this time? You were only a boy . . .'

'I was so scared I'd be punished. I couldn't get it out of my head that somehow I'd have to be punished for such a wicked thing. Everybody would know what I'd done, how I'd felt –

they'd see it in my face. My parents would realize, they'd never forgive me . . . Juliet would never forgive me.'

'Juliet?'

Ash shifted on the bed, turning so that he looked upwards, away from the girl beside him.

'Sometimes I think I see her out of the corner of my eye,' he said. 'I catch a shadow, a blur, and I turn and it's gone. But something lingers . . . I think I see her as she was then, a little girl, eleven years old, dressed in the same clothes as . . . as then.'

He closed his eyes, the image of Juliet sharp in his mind. But not her face. Her face had no solidity, no union of features. There was nothing there that could be focused upon. Further disturbed by the vagueness of his dead sister's countenance, Ash opened his eyes once more. 'The night before the funeral I heard her voice. She called to me. I was sleeping and her voice entered my dream. I woke and could still hear her, calling me to her. Her body was downstairs in an open coffin. I crept down there – I was so scared, but I couldn't resist, I had to see her. Maybe something in me wanted her to be alive again; probably I wanted my own guilt taken away.'

His breathing unsteady, he said: 'Juliet moved, Christina. Her body moved in that coffin. She spoke to me.'

As if fascinated, Christina watched him closely. He lolled his head towards her.

'It could have been a nightmare – I don't know. I was just a kid, I'd been through an awful experience. But something inside me told me it was really happening. My parents heard my screams. When they found me I was a heap on the floor. I'd passed out, fainted.'

His throat was dry, as though truly scorched by the dry heat in the cellar. His tongue moved across his lips, barely moistening them.

'I was in a fever for two weeks after that – I missed it all, the service, the funeral, the worst of the family grieving – and they put it down to the fall in the river. I'd caught a chill. Can you believe that? I was glad that's all they thought.'

Her hand reached for his. 'Oh, David,' she said, 'that's why, isn't it?'

Ash gave a slight shake of his head, not understanding.

'That's why you've dedicated yourself to psychic investigation, disproving the supernatural, discounting life after death. Haven't you realized that?' She squeezed his hand in insistence. 'Your scepticism comes from your own guilt. You never wanted there to be any such thing as ghosts. You were afraid of that nightmare, frightened that it hadn't been a dream, that Juliet *had* spoken, *had* moved in her coffin. You've always been afraid that it really happened, that your sister would somehow demand retribution. David, can't you see what a fool you've been?'

She moved closer, lifting herself so that she could kiss his cheek.

Ash held on to her, dismayed by her words, yet sensing there was some truth, some logic, to them. But it was too soon to accept such reasoning, for the unease had been with him too long, for too many years. He needed time to think. He needed to rest. He needed to consider her words. And at that moment, more than anything else, he needed Christina.

Ash groaned as he gathered her tight against him.

T W E N T Y - O N E

His eyelids fluttered open.

The room was in darkness save for soft moonlight through the window.

His naked body was wet with perspiration. His throat was parched. He remembered the fire.

He remembered everything.

Ash turned to Christina, wanting her reassurance, and as he moved he was aware that desire was still not satiated.

But Christina was not there. Her side of the bed was empty, and when he whispered her name there was no response from the shadows that cluttered the room.

The sheets where she had lain were drawn back, moonlight shading the indentation left by her body.

He touched that place, as if something of her presence might still be evoked; but the coldness he felt caused him to gasp and withdraw his hand.

It was as though his fingertips had dipped into icy liquid, for the chill was not only confined to the bedclothes themselves: an aura of frigidity seemed to issue from their rumpled surface.

He lay back, well away from that part of the bed, fear

renewed, his thoughts unclear; yet he was too weary for effort, too exhausted in spirit to rise.

His eyelids were overwhelmingly heavy.

TWENTY-TWO

Edith Phipps hurried up the short flight of steps leading into
the Psychical Research Institute, her cheeks pinched red by
the frosty morning air. Behind her, rush-hour traffic crawled
almost to a standstill, drivers venting their frustration on
steering wheels or travelling companions, but only occasionally on their horns. Through the glass panels of the building's
double-door, Edith caught sight of Kate McCarrick descending
the stairs leading from the Institute's offices. She pushed open
the door with some vigour, anxious to reach her colleague.

'Kate . . .' she said, once inside, a little out of breath.

The other woman expressed surprise, but continued her
journey towards the receptionist's desk. 'Hello, Edith. Sorry
I can't stop – I'm late for the conference.' To the receptionist,
Kate said, 'Did you get me a cab?'

'Outside waiting for you,' came the brisk reply.

'Terrif. These are for posting – must go off this morning.'
The research director laid a pile of envelopes on the
desk.

'Kate, I have to talk to you.' Edith was by Kate's elbow.

'No time, Edith,' Kate said, facing the flustered medium.
'I really am running late. I'll try and ring you later. Will you
be here at the Institute?'

'Yes, I've got three sittings this morning. But it's important . . .'

'So's the conference. There's a lot of introductions I have to make before it starts and I'll be skinned alive if I'm not there to do it.'

Politely as she could, Kate brushed past Edith, heading for the door.

The medium called after her. 'It's about David.'

Kate hesitated, one hand against the swing door, undecided. Then: 'We'll talk later.'

She went through, the door swinging shut behind her. Edith went after her, but stopped when she saw Kate through the glass climbing into the waiting taxi. The medium bit into her lower lip, knowing it would be useless to follow.

Instead she climbed the stairway, the effort tiring her more than she cared to admit, and made for Kate McCarrick's office.

Inside, she put her handbag on the research director's desk and went straight to a filing cabinet. She pulled out a drawer and studied the index of names.

Edith stopped when she found MARIELL. She took out the file.

As she opened it, she remembered the first time she had begun to wonder about David Ash . . .

TWENTY-THREE

'Edith, meet David Ash.'

The dark-haired man had risen from his chair as Edith had entered the room, and now he extended a hand. His reserve was obvious. Interesting face, she thought, the deepest of eyes . . .

A sensation ran through her, the kind of shiver that can be caused by brushing fingertips over velvet, when they touched hands. The mild shock interrupted her thoughts.

His grip relaxed as if he, too, were momentarily confused; the handshake became firm again. 'Kate has told me a lot about you,' he said.

'And I know of your reputation,' she replied, equally swift to collect herself. Edith returned his smile to let him know there was no animosity intended in the remark.

'I was surprised you asked Kate for my help.'

'Believe it or not,' said Kate McCarrick, beaming at them both, 'Edith admires your work.'

Ash raised his eyebrows.

'I don't doubt your motives, Mr Ash,' Edith said. 'There really *are* too many charlatans in my profession. We suffer enough public scorn without these people exposing us all to even more ridicule.'

Ash was direct. 'Forgive me for saying this, but I'm used to your kind closing ranks on me.'

'Not when we, ourselves, suspect fraud. It may take years, but such imposters are usually found out, and when that happens it reflects badly on us all. Their sharp practices need to be nipped in the bud, Mr Ash, to minimize the damage.'

'And before these bogus mediums gain too big a following,' Kate added. 'The bigger the fan club, the harder it is to discredit the idol.'

Ash knew the truth of that – like any religion (for many, clairvoyance was regarded as such), it was the devotees' *will* to believe that had to be confronted as much as the methods of the individual trickster.

'The particular person we want you to investigate is beginning to step beyond acceptable bounds,' said Kate.

'Beyond acceptable bounds?' Ash addressed his question to Edith: 'So there are some deceptions, if they're trivial enough, that are allowed?'

'I can't deny the theatrics of some mediums,' Edith replied, 'but they're harmless, just their way of inducing a mood for sensing.'

She hadn't liked Ash's smile then.

Kate stood up from her desk, wary of how the meeting was progressing. 'Why don't I rustle up some tea or coffee while you explain the case in point to David? I think he'll be very interested.'

'I believe you will,' said Edith as Ash sat and drew out a cigarette from its pack, his face expressionless. 'Yes, I really believe you will.'

It was impressive. The atmosphere was charged, the expectation almost tangible. The light was low in the huge room – not just dim, not just suitably muted for the occasion of a seance, but *low*, dramatically so.

Ash inspected the medium who stood alone some distance

away. She was impressive too, he mused. Jet-black hair (it *had* to be dyed that colour), drawn back severely over her scalp to gather into a tight bun at the nape of her neck; her heavily mascara'd eyes tilted at the corners as if from the strain of stretched skin. Sultry lips, darkly rouged, a prominent nose which dominated but did not spoil her face. Naturally enough, she was dressed in black: high-necked silk blouse, long, full skirt, and even dark hose and shoes. Value for money, Ash said to himself. If I were a paying customer (and he knew that money would change hands some time during the evening) it's what I'd expect as part of the show. Her name was Elsa Brotski and he wondered why she didn't go all the way and add the title 'Madame'. All very impressive, but ludicrous too. Yet she was obviously revered by her following.

He studied the eager 'guests' around him, women in the main, a few elderly or middle-aged men among them. It was the latter who appeared the quietest; a hushed, but considerably excited, murmuring came from the women.

Ash had never attended a seance of this size before. Spiritualist meetings were usually more crowded, although they were mostly held in halls which could be filled to capacity. But this was a private sitting and there were more than twenty-five people (not counting the medium and her aides) gathered there, all seated on benches that were arranged into a U-shape, the interior left empty, the medium herself seated alone on a chair at the open end.

As Ash studied the people around him, so Edith, seated on the opposite side of the U-formation, studied him.

Over the past few weeks, she had come to know him a little – *just* a little – and had begun to realize that his scepticism, misguided though it might be, was born out of a sincere yearning for truth. Not that he was on any kind of holy mission – there was certainly nothing evangelical about this man – for Ash's intellect was too complicated to allow anything so direct. She sensed that he was driven by something that he, himself, could not understand. *'It's a job, not a vocation,'* he had told her in one of their recent conversations, but she wondered then as she did now if that were really true. He wasn't an easy man to understand, and that was probably because he hardly understood himself; yet she sensed the frustration in him – no, it was something more, something deeper, than mere frustration: a personal desperate seeking perhaps? That might be wrong, too. She didn't know why, but Edith suspected it was quite the antithesis of that. What a strange notion on her part, she thought. Was it possible that a quest for truth could have its very denial as an underlying motive? Edith realized that her confusion about David Ash would not have been possible had not her mind occasionally touched his. There was a mystery in itself.

It was a lessening of whispered chatter rather than an increase that aroused Edith from her ruminations. She turned her attention towards the woman in black who sat alone and slightly away from her 'guests' and who had been silent until now, as if gathering her mental energies for the seance that was to follow. As two men joined her, standing behind the seated figure like guards rather than helpers, the 'medium' smiled almost imperiously at the congregation.

The murmuring ceased entirely when she spoke. 'Bless you for coming this evening. I do believe I can already feel the excitement of our loved ones on the other side. Yes, yes, they are all quite impatient to speak.' Her scanning of the assemblage was slow, as if she were taking in everyone present; the sitters stirred with pleasure and with a certain amount of trepidation.

Edith felt a small flush of shame on her cheeks as though she, herself, were part of this charade. Before, Ash had asked her why she had no doubts that this woman was a fake. 'A true sensitive can't help but know,' she had said, the ambiguity of her reply unintended. She had quickly realized the answer was hardly satisfactory and had added that this particular person had accepted too many financial rewards over recent years to be genuine, for gross profit from one's ability could never be acceptable to those with the 'gift'. Cashing in on something so unique wasn't the way, she had told him, referring to 'the way' as a spiritual path, not an attitude. He took the point; whether or not he accepted it was another matter.

There was another reason for doubting the probity of Elsa Brotski, Edith had gone on to explain, and it was simply that this so-called 'medium' was just *too* infallible. She never, absolutely *never*, failed in her endeavours to contact any particular spirit on the other side; and that really was not credible, for all sensitives had failures – probably more so than successes, if truth be told. Yet this woman appeared to have none. Rather bluntly, Ash had wondered aloud about professional jealousy, and Edith had reminded him that all she and the Institute were asking him to do was investigate the woman. Prove them right or wrong, nothing more than that.

Admittance to the seance had not proved difficult, for anyone was welcome, it seemed (and that puzzled Edith: phoney mediums usually gleaned as much information as possible from potential sitters, thus slyly arming themselves with knowledge that might be perceived as startling intuition on the occasion of the seance itself; yet neither she nor Ash had been approached or vetted). The only problem turned out to be the long waiting list of 'guests', for this woman was rapidly gaining a reputation as a clairvoyant *supreme*. Almost two months had elapsed before Edith and Ash had received separate invitations (they had used fictitious identities as a precaution) and she had had to invent excuses so that her visit would be rearranged to coincide with his. The long wait had its advantages, for it had given Ash time to investigate Elsa Brotski's background.

Edith caught the faint nod of Ash's head towards her as the wall lights were dimmed even lower. She heard the soft gasp of her neighbour, a middle-aged woman who smelled of powder and soap. A small spotlight picked out the 'medium', her skin pale and her lips blood-red under its glare. Although the room was not in total darkness, it was virtually impossible for the gathering's attention not to be drawn towards that circle of light, which was now softening, becoming dulled as if it, too, were sinking with Brotski into her trance.

Her lips, now like blood-bruises in the deadening light, parted as she sighed, the sound almost orgasmic. She lifted her hands and the two aides on either side stepped forward to hold them, they in turn reaching for the nearest sitters.

'Join me,' the woman whispered breathlessly and, as if on cue, the seated people linked hands. The palm of the elderly man seated on Ash's right felt dry and hard like summer bark, while that of the woman on his left was as clammy damp as butcher's meat. He mentally complimented Elsa Brotski on the effectiveness of her presentation and watched with interest as her head sank lower onto her chest, her breasts beginning to heave beneath the shiny blouse. Her eyes had been closed, but now they opened as she raised her head once more and called a name:

'Clare.'

A low huskiness tempered her voice when she repeated the name.

A shifting of someone two bodies down from where Ash sat, a timorous utterance.

'I have someone here on the other side who wishes to speak to Clare,' said Brotski. Then she tilted her head as if to speak to someone by her left shoulder: 'Yes, I know, Jeremy. Please be patient.' She faced the audience again. 'Make yourself known, Clare, we have many eager to speak to us this evening.'

Ash grimaced. She didn't waste time, this woman. A little theatre, then straight into the show.

'I think it's me,' someone said from the shadows.

Immediately another spotlight came into life and its beam hurried along the row of people with whom Ash sat, stopping when it came upon a woman who was literally on the edge of her seat, her mouth open, her eyes keen with excitement. She blinked against the sudden light, even though it was not strong.

Ash had never witnessed an individual sitter singled out this way before, and was intrigued.

'Jeremy wants you to stop worrying,' Brotski told the sitter. 'He's happy where he is, but he would like you to visit him this way more often, he has lots to tell you. Will you do that for Jeremy, Clare?'

Clare nodded eagerly, tearfully.

'He says to tell you he feels no more pain, not even from his leg. You both worried so much about that, didn't you, Clare?'

Another eager nod, tears trickling freely now.

'Jeremy will have more to say to you next time. Just don't worry, and now that you've made contact, don't leave it so long next time.'

'I won't,' said the sitter, her voice quivering throatily when she repeated, '*I won't . . .*'

Clever, if not very subtle, admitted Ash. One new recruit, perhaps a member for life – her natural life, anyway. Were there set dues, he wondered, or were contributions purely voluntary and at guests' discretion? It mattered little: emotionally satisfied customers were usually generous with their offerings.

'I have an elderly gentleman here with white hair and a rather lovely beard,' the 'medium' announced. 'He wishes to speak to someone called . . .'

And so it went on, the spotlight (which Ash noticed was operated by a shadowy figure standing beyond the 'medium' and who moved the mounted light from time to time for a better position) singling out each sitter when their turn for conversation with the 'other side' came around. The stage-management was clever but obvious; what puzzled the investigator was how the woman in black knew so much about her 'guests' and their departed loved ones. She had to have had information about them beforehand.

Brotski engaged her individual 'guests' seemingly at random, the spotlight picking them out each time, creating the impression that there were only two people present in the room of any significance. It was a very physical way of helping two minds concentrate on each other. The messages from the dead were mostly mundane – *visit the doctor about that persistent backache, dear, he'll put it right, you'll be holidaying abroad this year and you'll meet someone who'll have something very interesting to say to you, don't worry about me, I'm fine, tell Granny Rose that her Tom is here with me and he'll be ready to meet her when her time comes, I always loved you even though sometimes you thought otherwise and I still love you now, be careful of that new stove you've bought, you're quite right, those headaches are brought on by a leaky connection, please don't grieve for me any more, it's been five years, time to pick yourself up and get on with your life, but please come and talk to me again, yes, of course I miss you, that builder hasn't made a good job of the back porch, have it checked out, you're right about your boss, he doesn't like you, time you found yourself a new job, my girl* – but they were obviously deeply meaningful to the persons at whom they were directed judging by the responses, some tearful, some full of joy.

The very banality of the proceedings made it all the more convincing. Yet Ash was far from convinced.

Not everyone in the room had been served with news from beyond – and that included Edith and Ash, himself. Would the 'medium' provide such communication only for those on whom she already had information? If she dealt with a reasonable number of sitters, the others would still be impressed. Did it take two or three visits before the 'lines' were open, giving this woman and her aides time to gain a little background knowledge on her new followers? Ash wondered just who would engage him in conversation after this meeting broke up. Well, he was prepared for that; he had some nice bits of false information to gi–

The light had picked out Edith.

Ash was startled. They knew nothing about her, not even her real name. Why should the phoney medium, who was pointing at Edith as if she had directed the light, have singled out a stranger?

It seemed that a long silence had followed, although in reality it was no more than a few seconds. Edith shifted uncomfortably in her seat and looked across at Ash.

The other woman's face tightened into a grimace of rage. Then she shifted her gaze to the investigator.

Even though he was still in shadow, Ash felt vulnerable under her glare.

'*Get them out!*' Brotski shrieked.

Everyone present, and in particular, Edith and Ash, was shocked rigid by the vehemence of the outburst.

'*Those two!*' The 'medium's' hand wavered between the intruders.

One of the helpers hurriedly approached, peering into the gloom to locate the second interloper, and Ash rose from the bench, stepping over it, the flat of his hand held out to ward off the other man, who looked to have murder in his heart.

Ash swore under his breath. This wasn't the idea at all. He'd had no intention of having a public confrontation with the bogus medium; he'd planned to have a private word, warn her that unless she ceased her devious practices, he would expose her publicly as a fraud, giving full details of how she had duped her 'guests' as well as mentioning the wealth she had accrued in doing so. Such a threat had worked often enough in the past, for once found out, most charlatan clairvoyants found it nigh impossible to establish credibility thereafter. Better to retire gracefully, find some other form of chicanery.

So much for planning, Ash thought wryly as the aide drew nearer. He received a jolt that caused his body to sag briefly. Perplexingly, it was not a physical shove – the helper was still yards from him. Ash swung his head back to Brotski.

She was visibly trembling, her eyes blazing at him. He felt more than resentment pouring from her; there was loathing in that look – and there was fear. Fear of him. He felt it so strongly, so *powerfully*, and he could not understand how. It was not in the way someone might sense the disliking or distrust of another from the way in which that person acted; this hatred was *inside* Ash's own mind, as though her very look could invade his head. Ridiculously, he imagined *sci-fi* gamma-rays emitting from her eyeballs, punching through his skull, the *splat* of an exploding thought. At once he realized how this woman performed her tricks. And further realized that although she was a fake clairvoyant, in another sense she was very, very genuine.

Hands grabbed at him. 'Okay you – out, *now.*' The helper's voice was low, but there was no mistaking the menace.

Ash pushed the hands away. 'You don't talk to the spirits at all, do you?' he calmly said to the woman who was still seated at the end of the two rows, the spotlight giving full display to her fury. The other 'guests' were shifting in their seats in agitation, looking from their host to the man who was now speaking, then back again. Someone grumbled and others joined in. Their vexation was directed towards Ash.

'It's time these people were told how you manage to give such a good performance,' Ash went on, undaunted.

The helper tried to get hold of him again and Ash shoved him away more forcefully. 'You're gifted all right,' he said over the increasing babble of indignation, 'but not in the way you pretend.'

The second helper had begun to make his way towards the investigator.

'She's telepathic,' Ash said to the shadowy faces around him. 'She has a great gift, but she's using it to deceive unfortunate people like yourselves.' He hadn't been sure, although the assertion was not just a guess; her thoughts had pushed their way into his own and he had felt that in a very real way. But now her expression confirmed everything he had said, for it had become sly, her eyes skittish, darting from him to the people who were turning towards her. She resembled, and only for a moment, an animal at bay, one that had not yet lost its cunning.

'*No!*' someone shouted.

'She's using it to make money out of you,' Ash insisted.

There were more cries of denial, of disbelief, from the gathering.

'Listen to me,' Ash said patiently. 'I was sent here from the Psychical Research Institute to investigate this woman. Her claims of clairvoyance have been under suspicion for some time.' If Kate McCarrick had been present, she would have groaned aloud. This really wasn't the way the Institute cared to conduct its investigations, and in truth, Ash, himself, was surprised by his own lack – *slanderous* lack of discretion. Perhaps the threatening approach of the aides, who were acting more like 'minders', had provoked the outburst; or perhaps the vicious probing of the woman's thoughts (which somehow felt unclean, like a molesting) had shocked him to outrage.

'You're wrong. You don't know what you're talking about.' The protest came from one of the sitters and others around the man voiced their agreement.

'She's helped me,' another called out. 'She's given me peace of mind!'

'She's brought our son back to us!' cried someone else.

'No, she hasn't!' Ash insisted. 'She hasn't done anything of the kind. I've checked out her background and I can tell you she's not what she seems. Ask her about the cult religion she started nine years ago in Leeds, which closed down in such a hurry when police began to make enquiries about the strange goings on behind closed doors, rituals that required naked young girls to commit certain unsavoury acts with older men. Ask her about the widower in Chester who paid her handsomely every week for a handwritten letter from his dead wife.'

The protests from those around Ash grew in volume.

'Get her to explain why she had to leave Edinburgh in such a hurry,' he went on. 'The authorities there don't take kindly to *clairvoyants*' – he sneered the word – 'who persuade infirm old ladies to sign over their estates to them in the promise they'll be found a better home in the next world with all their long-departed friends and relatives there to greet them on the great day.'

'*Don't listen to this madman*,' Brotski hissed. 'Most of you know me, you know what I've done for you. Would you take his word against mine?' Still she sat as if rooted to her chair, her hands clenched whitely over the edges of the wood.

'Those of you who've been invited here before – how much have you paid for the privilege?' Ash asked. 'Think about it. Just how much has it cost you to talk to the dead?'

Now both helpers were upon him. They pulled at his arms, trying to propel him towards the door. He resisted and one of the men whispered close to his ear, 'If you know what's good for you, you'll go quietly. Yours won't be the first pair of legs I've broken personally.'

A rough hand clamped over Ash's mouth as he tried to reply. Angrily he brought his elbow back sharply into the softness below his assailant's chest and had the satisfaction of hearing an explosive wheeze. The hand over his mouth fell away.

'Someone turn the lights up,' an anxious voice demanded. 'I can't see what's happening there.'

But the lights remained dim. The only pool of brightness was that in which the black-clothed woman sat. And now, it was noticed by some, she was staring frozenly into the horseshoe of figures. Staring at one person in particular, even though that person was indistinct in the gloom.

Her mouth slowly dropped open. Her eyes hardened into a gawp of unease.

Others in the room became aware of the sudden hush.

It was almost a wail, nearly a lamentation. 'Nooooo . . .' said the woman in black. Everyone heard the low-moaned cry, and everyone became silent.

Hands still grasped Ash, but they were slack, powerless.

Ash recognized the next voice, even though he could barely see Edith Phipps among the sitters, the mobile spotlight now extinguished.

'*Leave us in peace,*' Edith said in a harsh whisper that somehow carried around the room as if the words had been shouted.

Ash shook himself free of the man holding him, meeting no resistance at all. No one moved. The voice from the shadows had an uncanny quality, as if the message had been whispered by someone standing close to every individual in the room. Yet still they were aware it belonged to someone among the 'guests', someone seated on one of the benches.

Someone who was breathing in terrible dry gasps.

The voice again: *'We're nothing to you, leave us alone.'* A woman's voice . . . that somehow wasn't.

One of the sitters screamed, a short, piercing sound; she felt as if something terribly gelid had brushed by her, then passed on its way.

'We don't want to be here, not with you.' A subtle change in the voice, although it remained intrinsically the same, was still the unseen woman's. *'You can't use us this way, it torments us, it draws us back.'*

'Edith?' said Ash, stunned. He could see her shape, could make out the rise and fall of her plump shoulders; her face was shaded though, her features obscure.

She spoke again, although it was hardly her voice at all this time, the gruff tones masculine and raised in anger. *'Let them remember us as we were. It's wrong of you, don't . . .'*

'. . . don't you understand? It's so wrong of you!'

Heads turned as one towards the dark-clothed 'medium' under the spotlight, for it was she who was now talking, the voice that of the man who had spoken through Edith Phipps. Her eyes were moving without coordination, like a blind person's; her tongue flicked over rouged lips, wetting them, making them glisten.

'You're interfering with things you don't understand,' the voice continued. Her mouth formed shapes, but they bore little relation to the sounds that emerged.

Ash turned back to Edith to find she had slumped on the bench, the person beside her holding on, preventing her from slipping to the floor.

'You must stop, you . . . I can't see you, Mummy . . .' The voice had changed mid-sentence, had belonged to a child, girl

or boy, it was impossible to tell. Brotski rocked in her chair. *'Come and fetch me, Mummy, don't leave me here . . .'*

Someone in the crowd sobbed, a wretched, racked sound. 'It's my baby . . .'

'She's trying to fool you,' Ash said loudly, pointing accusingly at the dark woman.

Another voice followed on from that of the child: *'We're happy, we're happy . . .'*

The child's again: *'I want to come home to my own room . . .'*

Now an older person, a female's voice, cackling like a crone: *'I can see you, I can see you all . . .'*

And then the discarnate utterances intermingling, so many now, rushing against each other as though some incorporeal sluice-gate had been loosened, the voices flowing, tumbling through, some raised, anxious to be heard, others quiet, mannered, the sounds becoming a clamour, indistinct from each other, the whole moulding together like some sound engineer's experiment with a tape-deck, a cacophony of meaningless noise, a dissonant roar that made no sense at all . . .

'. . . without me your brother sends christmas no hurting any more I can't see you what if tell martha no why are please stop this if you look under the stair carpet what year mummy come and fetch me don't listen to her we never forget you over on this side I was glad no more sorrow here when will I david so many things to I can see you all that person will do you harm mummy please I'll wait I'll wait you there is grandad is whatever can it there is god don't grieve any be happy help one day stop this stop this stop this . . .!'

The last words were screamed.

Edith's body jerked, her eyes snapped open. She raised her head, looked over at the bright beam of downward light. She felt – she actually *felt* – the sensation of blood draining from her face.

The bogus medium was struggling to rise from her chair. But it seemed some unseen force held her there. Her back was arched, her hands were pushing against the wooden edges, knuckles strained in jagged, white-topped ridges. The whites of her eyes had become dominant around her pupils, as though invisible fingers were pulling back the lids, and her mouth yawned wide, the lips that had been lush suddenly thin and stretched; her cheeks had hollowed so that even under the glare of the spotlight there were faint shadows.

A fine mist had begun to drift from her mouth, a vapour that suggested that the air around her had frozen; but Edith had witnessed the emergence of ectoplasm, that physical representation of astral bodies, from the orifices of mediums on other, though rare, occasions. She was certain that this was the beginning of such, the stream as yet too tenuous, too weak, to create a definite shape.

The babbled words still came, although they had faded, were no longer loud, had levelled to a weary entreaty. And they were delivered while the woman's mouth remained locked open, carried by the vapour, neither her tongue nor her lips forming the sounds.

'*Stop this stop this stop . . .*'

The gentle expellation of mist faded, wisped away, but still there was a passing of shadows over her face, a curious shifting of light that subtly altered her features, changing her appearance yet never settling, an emphasis of cheekbone, perhaps a strengthening of the jaw, a furrowing of her brow; transient shapings, hints of different personalities, but nevertheless only a crawling of shadows beneath a still light.

The people around her, those guests who had held her in awe, could no longer control their panic. There were shouts of alarm, a furore of voices that overwhelmed the murmurings exhaled (it seemed) from her taut mouth.

The young woman who thought she had heard her dead child calling to her fought to get through to the seated 'medium', but others in the room had no further desire to stay and she was pushed, sent stumbling over a bench.

Two other women, both whimpering like frightened children, rushed past Ash, knocking him sideways in their desperation to leave. Others followed them in a mêlée of jostling bodies, all hurrying to reach the door, and although the bogus medium had become a distressing sight, Ash could not understand the acuteness of their terror. Surely they realized she was victim of some peculiar kind of fit? Then he realized that this woman (and now he acknowledged she was psychic, although his deep-rooted scepticism rejected any notion that she was clairvoyant) was somehow mentally projecting her own fear, the atmosphere itself charged with it. It spread like a rapid disease, touching, infecting everyone present, including himself. If he hadn't understood the absurd logic of it all, he too, would be heading for the exit. My God, he thought, no wonder they were in awe of her.

He flinched as a hand touched his arm.

'David, she's in terrible danger,' said Edith urgently.

He was relieved that Edith Phipps had recovered from her faint and relieved, too, that she showed no signs of panic. 'It's self-induced,' he said to her. 'I've seen this kind of hysteria before.'

She looked at him as though he were mad. 'No, it isn't that. We have to help her before it's too late. We have to bring her out of her trance.'

The crowd around them had thinned, most of the people now bunched around the door, jostling to get through. Edith and Ash had a clear view of the woman in the chair.

'Dear God,' breathed Edith.

Not everyone had rushed away. A few, just a few, including the Brotski aides, stood as if mesmerized by the sight before them. Somebody moaned. There was the crash of someone else collapsing to the floor.

For Elsa Brotski's face could hardly be called her own any more.

Its flesh heaved, rippled. The skin wrinkled into lines and whorls and just as abruptly there were smoothly clear patches, areas so fine they were nearly translucent. These transformations could no longer be mistaken for the shifting of shadows across her face, for the fleshy contortions were plainly evident. It was as if other countenances – *many* other countenances – existed beneath the surface, and each one was striving to announce itself, pushing from within, expanding the covering skin to its limit. It was an incredible and quite horrific spectacle; and it was nauseatingly fascinating.

It seemed that Elsa Brotski's face must surely burst.

Shocked, almost beguiled, Ash waited for the rapid transfigurations to run their course, cold-bloodedly, and even perversely, curious to see how far the phenomenon could progress, how it would end. There was little pity in him for the woman, and he could not help but despise himself for that.

He sensed Edith leaving his side and raised a hand to stop her, knowing where she was going. Her silhouette blocked the bizarre sight from his view, then she, too, was under the light, centre-stage in the nightmare.

She reached down for the tormented woman, laying her hands on the undulating face. She began to speak softly to her.

Ash made his way towards them, easing past those who had remained to watch with weird dread in their eyes. The helper whom Ash had pushed away earlier turned at the investigator's approach, but made no attempt to stand in his way. Instead, he backed off himself, hastily joining the throng around the exit. His colleague seemed struck rigid, unable or unwilling to go near the helpless woman. The third aide, the one who had operated the moveable spotlight that had singled out individual sitters, clutched the tripod as if for support, his head shaking in disbelief.

Edith staggered as Brotski suddenly lifted herself, her body arching outwards as if sprung, her hands still clenched around the edges of the chair, fastened there. She stretched herself in a perfect bow shape, her stomach enormously rounded as though in the final stages of pregnancy, her back hollowed. Yet her head was upright, resting on the shiny black material covering her breasts, giving the illusion that it had been disconnected from her neck and placed there. Worst of all were her eyes, for the pupils had rolled back inside their sockets so that only the whites showed, oddly swollen and lacklustre, like those of a grilled fish.

She presented an awful and terrifying vision, her features still not having settled, continuing to move in gargoylean patterns.

And the voices persisted, an unearthly gabbling that spilled from unmoving lips, a low outpouring of inanities – and anger . . .

'. . . can't if mind the cat you I it's different still remember that time won't long long tunnel ever bright light at mummy please mummy flowers here lots stop this leave tell everybody you the end death can't alone all pain ends don't forget under the stairs when you stop come over we don't wish this we want to I can see be left . . .'

Blood began to trickle from Brotski's nose; then from the corners of her eyes.

Ash stepped before her, made afraid by the sheer force of this woman's convulsions. Not knowing what else to do, he stooped and took her head in his hands as Edith had done, fighting the repulsiveness of that swelling, agitated flesh against his palms.

Her stomach and pelvis brushed against him in lascivious parody of seduction. The red-veined, leaking eyes glowered sightlessly at him. Her breath was foul, as though the words carried their own stinking effluence.

The fitful spasms seemed to concentrate themselves into a trembling, a shaking of her whole body that threatened to loosen Ash's grip on her face. Her spine curved even more, to the point it would surely snap, so that her belly quivered against his chest. Her head sat between her breasts like some grotesque palpitating effigy.

A one word litany could now be heard above the others . . .

'. . . stop . . . stop . . . stop . . .'

It was as though the violent quivering had reached its zenith, for Elsa Brotski suddenly solidified.

Or at least, that was how it felt to Ash. He might well have been holding on to a marble statue, so hard and frozen did the woman feel.

The voices had ceased. But a high-pitched keening had

replaced them, the sound distant, coming from deep inside the woman.

It grew, became piercing, erupting from the gaping hole that was her mouth as a deafeningly shrill shriek.

And then one more word. A name. Before Elsa Brotski fell unconscious into a loose, fluid heap.

Leaving Edith Phipps to wonder why David's name had been called, once among the babble of other voices and now as a single last cry.

TWENTY-FOUR

Ash stirred in the bed, one hand sliding across his forehead
to soothe away the pressure inside. He swallowed to ease
his parched throat. His eyes opened grudgingly. He drew in
a long draught of air as though breathing were not the most
natural thing.

He moved again, pushing himself up in the bed, that movement sluggish, almost drugged. Muted daylight shone through
the window to render shadows, those which at night had been
an intense and secretive umbra, no more than an insubstantial
shading. Ash murmured something, perhaps a protest against
his own lack of vitality.

With considerable effort he raised his wrist to study his
watch. Surprise played its part in overcoming the lethargy.
It was late afternoon; Ash had slept through most of the
day.

He leaned back against the headboard, wiping his hands
across his face to dispel the grogginess, then down across his
chest. His body felt grimed, staled, and he remembered how
soaked it had been when he'd woken during the dark hours.
Ash tugged the sheets away, unmindful of the room's low
temperature. His skin was dry now, pale in the daylight. The
bedclothes beside him were tangled, any indication of anyone

else having lain there since erased by his own troubled sleep. But there were semen stains on the sheet.

He rose from the bed, slow in action, a dullish pain loitering behind his eyes, and went to the window. Hands resting against the frame, he looked out at the gardens.

Everything was still. There was no breeze, no drifting of clouds (for the sky was blanket grey once more, sombre in its fullness), no sounds to be heard.

Even the house, even Edbrook, seemed strangely quiescent.

Ash was aware of all this, though his thoughts were directed inwards and were of the night before. He saw Christina, pure and beautifully white in her nakedness, dark hair loose around her face, her shoulders, the longest strands falling against the rise of her breasts. He touched her again in his mind and remembered her sensual response; again he felt her moistness, sensed her pleasured shudder.

Ash turned from the window and sat for a moment on the edge of the bed, his face pressed into his hands. Where had she gone? Why had Christina left him in the middle of the night?

He dressed slowly, without washing first – somehow the thought of cleansing himself never even entered his head. At the door he paused, hand resting on the handle. He waited there and wondered why he was reluctant to go out into the corridor. Ash realized that the very stillness of the house was unnerving him, for it seemed to hold a brooding quality, as though the timbers, the mortar, the house's *essence*, were waiting . . . For what? He was annoyed at himself. David Ash, the ultimate pragmatist, was now indulging in fantasy, and a foolish one at that. Edbrook was just a house. No more than that. With a tragic history, to be sure, and one so strong that possibly it could still project its image long after the event. But that had little to do with haunting in the truest sense. There were no ghosts here, no spectres, nor spirits, to bother the living. Perhaps Edbrook entertained trickery though.

With that thought in mind, the investigator pulled open the door.

The corridor was empty, and he hadn't expected it to be otherwise. That was the eerie thing – the house itself felt empty. Empty of life. Yet still . . . pensive.

Ash went along the dim corridor, passing the galleried stairway, glancing over into the well of the hallway as he did so. The very air inside Edbrook seemed heavy, aged. Perhaps the atmosphere had more to do with his own condition than actuality, for the previous night's trauma – *and* that of the first night – had left him weary and depressed. Even though he had slept most of the day away, there was a lassitude to his step and a muzziness inside his head that was difficult to dismiss.

He reached Christina's room and tapped lightly on the door. There was no reply. Ash didn't bother to knock again: he entered.

He stood at the doorway, mouth open slightly, his gaze roving.

There was nothing unusual about Christina's bedroom. The bed, with its brass head and foot rail, was neatly made, its feather quilt barely ruffled. Ornaments on old furniture were arranged tidily. Patterned curtains were tied back with splendid bows, decorative net diffusing the window light.

Nothing unusual about the room, except . . .

. . . Except that everything was too orderly – no magazines or books, no clothing, night attire or otherwise, lay scattered or draped over chairs – and everything was dulled, faded. As if the room and its contents were tempered by dust.

There was no vibrancy here, no indication of occupancy. Christina's bedroom had all the vitality of an unattended museum.

Resting on a bureau beneath an oval mirror were two silver-framed photographs and Ash moved closer to examine them. He picked up one and wiped dust from its glass: he recognized the sepia-toned couple from the portrait he had come upon the night before. Christina's parents, in formal pose, smiled frozenly and somewhat bleakly for the camera. The group in the second photograph, which had obviously been taken in more recent times, was the Mariell offspring. He was about to pick it up when he caught sight of his own reflection in the mirror, a light screen of dirt weakening the image; even so, he could discern the puffiness beneath his eyes, the darkness of his stubbled chin. Disconcerted, Ash moved away, brushing fingers through his tousled hair in token gesture of grooming.

He touched the bed, not knowing why (but perhaps in the way someone might caress their absent lover's clothing in surrogate intimacy), trailing his fingertips across the padded quilt. The material felt stiffened, its softness somehow brittle.

Leaving the bedroom, Ash went back to the stairway and descended hurriedly, anxious now and disturbed by the unnaturalness of the silence around him. He went from room to room, checking for any broken seals or powdered footprints before entering, and inside switching off detectors triggered by his own appearance.

With considerable trepidation, he approached the cellar, and it was from the top step that he checked for fire damage. Apart from the lumpy dust cover, beneath which lay the shattered brandy bottle, there was no evidence of anything having happened down there: no blackened walls, no charred timbers, no lingering stench of smoke. It had all been an illusion. The files at the Psychical Research Institute were full of such. Ash was not sure whether he felt relief or dismay.

From the cellar he walked down the hallway to the kitchen and here he stopped before going through. There were noises coming from inside. Faint sounds. A scratching.

The door was ajar and Ash pushed it further open with the flat of his hand, the pressure soft, cautious.

The mice on the kitchen table were unaware of his presence until the door came to the end of its slow swinging arc to bump against a unit behind. The tiny creatures scuttled without even bothering to glance at the intruder, some leaping onto a chair pushed in at the table, others running down (impossibly it seemed) the table's legs.

Ash felt his skin crawl at the sight of them, with their furry bodies and trailing worm-like tails. There had been perhaps a half-dozen on the table top, but there might well have been hundreds such was the nauseating effect on him. The ravaged bread – half a loaf, a grey-bladed knife lying nearby – they had feasted upon was pockmarked with black mould. The sight of it, together with the after-image of those busy creatures smothering its surface, set Ash's stomach to heaving.

He headed for the sink, hoping, although at that moment not caring too much, he wouldn't step on one of those tiny fleeing bodies. It was bile only, and not undigested food, that spattered the backs of two cockroaches in the sink, and he shrank away, swallowing back the sour juices that continued to rise. *Dear God, the place was filthy! What had happened overnight at Edbrook?* Of course, even if the question had been voiced and was not just a yell inside his head, there appeared to be no one around to answer him. He reached for the tap and twisted the old-fashioned cross head. Brown water spurted and clunked in the pipes like caught metal before running smoothly and becoming clear. The black beetles swilled around with his bile, their thread-legs frantic paddles. He turned off the tap and walked away from the sink, trusting the subsequent whirlpool to suck them away.

The back door was unlocked and he stepped outside, relieved to be in the open, wintry though it was. He wiped the wetness from his lips and chin with the back of his hand and took in deep gulps of air, some of his tiredness instantly vanishing. He shivered with the cold and then, almost desperately, he called Christina's name.

Had he really expected an answer? Ash couldn't be sure. Nevertheless, he called again.

He listened to the silence.

From the terrace overlooking the gardens, he cupped both hands around the circle of his mouth.

'*Chriiistiiinaaa . . .!*'

Once more he called, but with less effort this time, and with little heart.

Christina had left Edbrook. And so too, it seemed, had Nanny Tess. Ash was alone, and he wondered why he so foolishly imagined that the decaying house behind him was gloating.

T W E N T Y - F I V E

The red Fiesta eased itself cautiously into the motorway's traffic flow, headed in a north-westerly direction, picking up speed quickly as if joyous to be free finally of the congested city streets.

But there was no joy on the face of the bright vehicle's sole occupant. And it was not wariness of speeding juggernauts that caused Edith Phipps to grip the steering wheel so tightly.

Ash pulled on his overcoat as he walked along the corridor towards the stairs, not even taking time to close the bedroom door after him. He descended swiftly, wanting to be clear of this place, this empty abode whose brooding gloom oppressed the spirit. The sharp air outside had done something at least to shake off his lethargy and his intention now was to move fast before the reviving effect waned.

At the bottom of the stairs he hesitated. He looked back along the hallway at the black monstrosity of a telephone. One more try, he decided. Nothing to lose save a few seconds. He went to the instrument and lifted the heavy receiver to his ear. It was hardly a smile, but the corners of his mouth twitched upwards. The phone was dead, as he knew it would be.

He dropped the receiver the last couple of inches onto its cradle, then wiped dust from his hand with the sleeve of his coat.

His footsteps clattered on the wood floor as he hastily made his way to Edbrook's entrance. Ash opened one half of the double-door, stepped through, and descended the three stone steps outside scarcely breaking stride.

He tugged the collar of his coat upright, folding a lapel across his chest to ward off the chill breeze. His feet crunched noisily against the gravel of the pitted drive.

So dangerously close did the articulated lorry sweep by the Fiesta that Edith was afraid she and her vehicle might be sucked beneath its huge wheels. As it was, the slipstream of the giant's wake buffeted the car so that her hands had to grip the steering wheel even more tightly to keep control.

A glance in her wing mirror told her the lorry had its junior cohorts close behind, vehicles whose drivers' patience had probably been discarded the moment their machines' wheels had touched three-lane concrete. She checked her own speed. Fifteen below the limit. Perhaps the fault was hers, then. Still, she wasn't alone at 55 mph. 'And just look at us,' she mumbled scornfully, 'bunched together like a convoy of hearses.' A cheerless simile – and how it suited her mood. Why this awful debilitating dread, Edith? Why this irrational fear for David? Impossible to answer. 'Second' sight did not mean 'clear' sight. Mostly there were only feelings, intuitions; but oh, this was so *strong*, so overwhelmingly *strong*! And it came from David himself. He was the link. It was as if the poor man were sending out a distress signal. But it was blurred, so confused . . .

Her foot touched the brake as she realized she was mere yards away from the car in front.

Calm yourself, she ordered. Whatever was wrong, whatever was going on at this house called Edbrook, she would be of no use to David if her body were splattered across the motorway. Good Lord, such morbid thoughts! And bad for you, Edith, she admonished. Very, *very* bad for you.

Edith risked looking down at the road-map book lying open on the passenger seat. She did not want to miss the motorway exit and the road which would lead to another road, which would lead her to yet another road, which would eventually lead her to the Ravenmoor area.

Watchful of the way ahead again, she shifted the two letters obscuring the relevant map page, letters signed by Miss T. Webb, then quickly checked the correct exit number.

'A long way yet,' she murmured to herself, and flinched as another lorry thundered by.

Once inside the telephone box, Ash gave himself time to recover his breath before ringing the Institute. At least the walk from Edbrook along the country lanes had cleared his head. He felt sharper, and somehow more vigorous despite the hike; perhaps all he had needed to throw off the mental tiredness was fresh air and brisk exercise. He blamed the house itself, with all its staleness and dismal light for his earlier condition. And the traumas of the past couple of nights, he reminded himself. The Mariells were playing games with him, trying to discredit him, and he didn't know why. Did he care? Did he really give a damn about what they were up to? Curiously, he did. What he wasn't sure of, though, was whether he cared *enough*. They disturbed him, the Mariells; and perversely, he had to admit, they fascinated him. Especially Christina. Last night . . .

He stopped himself. He needed some sanity brought into the situation, some direction. He needed to talk to McCarrick; solid, sensible and logical Kate.

Ash dug deep into his pockets. He swore when he brought out pennies only.

He pushed open the heavy door and stepped out onto the grass. He looked behind him, back down the lane towards Edbrook.

But when he started walking, it was in the opposite direction.

This was the one, this was the exit from the motorway that she wanted.

Edith indicated left and soon was relieved to leave the fast-lane lemmings for the quieter country roads. At a more comfortable speed she passed through towns and villages, pleased to come upon the open stretches of countryside, to see the soft hills in the distance.

The first lights began to blink on as the day dulled to dusk.

Ash's stride had lost any briskness by the time he reached the outskirts of the village; his shoulders were slumped, his eyes cast down at the roadway, the two-mile journey having all but drained him of his newfound (and swift to diminish) vigour.

The houses became more regular, less of a stutter, some now joined at the hip, soon running into terraces along the high street. Lights inside were being switched on, and here and there he glimpsed the warm glow of firesides. There was something irresistibly comforting about these homes, a soothing reassurance for the lone traveller; yet that very cosiness also served to emphasize the isolation of the outsider. Ash felt completely alone.

The puffs of white air he breathed before him dissolved around his face, as insubstantial as fleeting thoughts; the evening's bitterness was countered by the exertion of his body. He passed by shops, their larger brightness harsh to his eyes; but in the distance was a more welcoming light.

His pace increased a fraction and his throat seemed drier in anticipation.

Edith stood next to the Fiesta as the elderly pump attendant filled the tank, grumbling to her about the nights drawing in, winter comin' on, lack of decent summers, and the price of meat (it was a small garage on a B road, and pumping fuel wasn't the most interesting job in the world although it at least gave occasion for conversation with itinerant customers).

Oh yes, Ravenmoor weren't far, not far at all, and yes he knew of a place called Edbrook, a big old house, lotsa ground 'round it, and no, that weren't far neither, less'n three miles further on, before you got to the village, and no, he weren't sure who lived there, not the name anyways, the place was sort of there an' weren't there, if you know what I mean, just a house set back off the road with no nearby neighbours and the folk – whoever they were – kept to themselves, not that he would know them anyways (he chuckled here) because he was a new boy in these parts, only moved to the area with his second wife – widowed again two years later – ten or 'leven years since and anyways he had no cause to socialize with people who lived in big places like that although a lady who *did* live there stopped by for petrol every so often in one of them lovely ol' cars, in perfect nick it looked, as if it weren't taken out much, and he knew she came from there because once she'd had no cash and had to pay him by cheque and he'd had to ask her to jot down her address, blowed if he could 'member her name now, but she never said much when she called in, weren't one for a chat, not like him, he enjoyed a good jaw, and if you foller the road, missus, take the secon' right, then watch for the first small lane left, foller it round 'til you hit a bigger, but not too big, road, hang a left (his six-year-old grandson in Plymouth had taught him that one), then Edbrook was just a bit further on.

He paused for breath and another chuckle.

Knew the place, oh yes, and didn't care much for it. Passed it a few times and got bad vibes (his grandson had taught him that one, too). When you were into your seventies – yep, seventy-two and still working, afternoons and odd evenings, mebbe, but still at it, wouldn't want it no different – when you were into your seventies you got feelings 'bout such things, know what I'm saying, missus? You get to *know*. There you go, full to the brim an' ready to race, need a bill for the tax man? no? then I'll get your change, how about oil? you okay for oil? no, these little tin cans never drank the oil like the big old brutes used to, still that's progress, so they say, though I reckon some things have *re*gressed, if you know what I mean, things aren't the same no more, but times don't stand still an' you gotta keep up . . .

To Edith's relief, the attendant went off to his office of whitewashed stone and she called after him to keep the change. She was already sliding into the driver's seat and reaching for the safety belt before he had time to turn around and wave her a thanks.

The landlord of the Ravenmoor Inn had barely opened the door to sample the evening's climate (cold wasn't a problem, nor even icy, but rainy tended to keep the punters – save for the die-hards – indoors) when the dark-coated man virtually stumbled into him. No local lad, this one, and a bit untidy. A clean shave wouldn't have hurt his appearance. He stepped back to allow the customer across the threshold.

Ash mumbled an apology as he brushed by the landlord. He made his way through the vestibule into the saloon bar, while his host took his time in following.

'Cold evening,' the landlord offered in conversation as he strolled around the bar counter.

Ash merely nodded in agreement and pointed at the row of spirits inverted over optics behind the other man. He singled out the vodka bottle.

'A large one,' he said. 'A *bloody* large one.'

Edith slowed the car, her face close to the windscreen as she peered at the gate-posts ahead. She switched her headlights to full-beam in order to see more clearly.

Yes, this was the place, for as she drew closer she could just discern the name EDBROOK etched into the brick pillars on either side of the drive. The gates were drawn back and she pulled off the road, bringing the Fiesta to a halt inside. In the evening light she was able to make out the shadow of a large house at the end of a long, straight driveway. There were no lights on inside the house.

She sensed nothing.

It could have been an empty shell down there.

'David . . .' she said quietly, as if the whisper could rouse him at such a distance.

No, she sensed nothing. Yet she had no desire to enter that darkly unhappy place. If only David . . .

Edith eased her foot from the brake and drove onwards.

Lawns soon spread out on either side, woods beyond them, and then there were gardens. In the half-light she could not tell if they were well-tended. She gasped – for a moment she had thought there were people standing in the grounds, but she quickly realized that their sinister stillness had the frigidity of stone. She ignored the impression that these statues were observing her approach.

The house grew larger in the windscreen, soon filling the view completely, the car's headlights brightening its façade, but only to dreariness.

She parked the vehicle beneath a tree whose branches overhung the gravelled yard in front of Edbrook, and some distance away from the steps leading up to the house's entrance. A safe distance away, she taunted herself, embarrassed by her own lack of nerve. She regarded the edifice with uneasy curiosity, wondering why it could make her feel so, for still she sensed nothing, no hint at all of its history, nothing of what was contained within those stained walls.

Then why the fear? It was there, deep inside her like some small rotting core, a cancered cell quietly corrupting others around it with almost somniferous slowness, working its way through her system, growing horribly towards fulfilment, encouraged by forces outside . . . outside but inside this grim house . . .

There, Edith, she told herself. You do sense something. An awful clutching blankness, whose root cause was very real. There was horror here and David Ash had become part of it.

Edith had set out on this journey with enough resolve to counter her trepidation, her purpose being to warn David of the danger surrounding him, a threat rendered obscure to him by the self-denial of his own gift. It was as if the sensing, unable to break through whatever psychological blockage he, himself, had imposed, this tenuous yet unyielding barrier between the conscious and the subconscious, had chosen another route. No, not quite right. The part of him that mediated between what he believed in and that which, through logic, he rejected, this intrinsic arbitrator common to us all (or nearly all, she had to modify) – which might be termed perception – had been forced to send off these thoughts in another direction. Edith was the one who had collected them, as the arbitrator had hoped she would. David had beaconed his own distress signal and probably wasn't even aware (oh, the fun a psychoanalyst could have with a mind like David's). And now the trepidation had seriously subjugated her resolve.

Edith considered turning the car around and driving away from this unpleasant place. There appeared to be no one at home, anyway; no lights were on. Perhaps David had already returned to London, his investigation completed. Perhaps her fears were in error. No, no, she resisted. Supposition could be argued against, sensing couldn't be. If David really had left, all well and good. If there was no one at home, perhaps even better – she could leave in the knowledge that at least she had been willing.

Still she felt nothing from the house itself. It was as though only a void was within its shelter, that clutching blankness perplexing to her. But if there was truly nothing there, then there was no need to be afraid. Nothing was nothing to be afraid of, was it, Edith?

She opened the car door. She shivered. She crossed the gravelled yard. She mounted the three broad, stone steps.

One half of the double-door was ajar, the wedge of shadow in the gap as black as velvet.

Edith jabbed the bell button set in the wall beside the entrance. When no sound came from inside the house, she pushed hard, leaving her stiffened finger there for several seconds. Still no ringing.

She rapped on the closed side of the double-door, knuckles instantly reddening with the force she used. When again there was no response, Edith reached in and swung the other door wide. The black velvet barely retreated.

'Hello?' she called, poking her head inside. 'Hello? Can anyone hear me?' She almost smiled: she had nearly asked, 'Is there anybody there?'

Her head flinched as the stench hit her, a noxious smell of age and damp and . . . and other things. Oddly, one of those things was charcoal.

Curious, Edith slid sideways through the open doorway.

Because it was dusk, it did not take long for her eyes to adjust to the inkiness of Edbrook's interior. It was as if parts of the velvet had become threadbare.

'Oh dear God . . .' she said under her breath.

And further along the spacious hall, from a doorway beneath the stairs, a shadow rose as if summoned by her quiet cry.

TWENTY-SIX

Ash leaned both elbows on the bar and showed his empty glass to the landlord. 'Another large one,' he said.

The landlord took the glass, eyeing the man warily. Drinking for this one wasn't just a social event: it had a more serious intent. He turned his back on Ash and pushed the glass under the vodka optic. 'And a bitter, too?' he asked over his shoulder.

Ash stubbed out his cigarette in an ashtray. 'Why not? I'm not driving.'

The inn had more customers now, although it was far from full; the night was too bleak to stray far from home comforts. Conversations were low-key, a general murmuring broken only by the muted cries of frustration or elation from the darts-players in the smaller and starker public bar next door.

The vodka was put before Ash and his empty pint glass taken away. The landlord pulled the bitter pump, watching the dishevelled man as he did so. 'You say you're staying locally . . .?' he ventured.

Ash dipped his hand into the ice bucket. 'Local enough. A bloody long walk though.' He dropped ice into the vodka.

'Out of the village then, is it?' The landlord slowly eased up on the pump.

'Yeah, about a hundred miles.' Ash summoned up a weary grin to show the other man he was joking. 'No – a couple of miles, I think. It just feels like a hundred. Out at Edbrook. You know it?'

'Edbrook?' the landlord said with mild interest. 'Yes, I know the place.'

'With the Mariell family.' He shook his head, smiling to himself.

The landlord put the pint on a mat and leaned forward on the bar. 'Out of the way little spot all right. You staying there long?'

'Not if I can help it.' He handed over two pound coins. 'I'm thinking of getting the train back to London tonight, as it happens. If it wasn't for . . .' He shrugged and took a swallow of vodka.

'So you're not enjoying your visit?' said the landlord conversationally and was surprised at his customer's grim laughter.

Ash shook his head, grinning a drunk's grin. 'I suppose you might call the Mariells eccentric.'

'The Mariells?'

'Yeah, all of them. Robert and Simon, dear old Nanny Tess. Even . . . even Christina.'

The landlord straightened and his tone became less than friendly. 'Maybe you ought to take it easy on the vodka. If you've got to get back there tonight . . .' He left the sentence unfinished as he went to the till. When he placed Ash's change on the bar he added, 'Of course, if that *is* where you're staying.'

With that the landlord walked away leaving the investigator to frown after him. Ash shrugged again and drank from the pint glass. He sifted through the coins before him with one finger. Picking up a 10p, he drained the vodka and left the bar; his journey across the saloon may not have been unsteady, but it was concentrated upon.

Outside in the vestibule he went to the public telephone, balanced the coin on its appropriate slot and lifted the receiver. He dialled a number and waited.

'Come on, Kate,' he muttered to himself after a while, 'where are you when I need you?'

Still no one answered at the other end. He sighed impatiently and leaned against the wall, aware that he had been swaying.

At Kate McCarrick's apartment a key was turning in the front door as the telephone shrilled its double bleep. The door opened and Kate hurried in, dumping her briefcase on the hallway floor as she headed for the phone.

She snatched up the receiver. 'Hello?' she said breathlessly.

There was a *click* as the line went dead at the other end.

Kate scowled. 'Sh–'

–it!' cursed Ash as he slammed down the receiver.

He slumped back, head against the wall, face raised towards the ceiling. He rubbed his forehead and eyelids with his fingers, then stayed there unmoving for several moments, his temples pounding from fatigue and the alcohol consumed. *Leave them to it, Ash,* he told himself. *Let them play their bloody games with someone else. What the hell does it matter to you?*

'Yeah, what the hell,' he mumbled aloud.

Was he over-reacting? Was he merely angry because Christina had gone from Edbrook without leaving any message for him, no acknowledgement of the intimacy they had shared the night before? He remembered her hunger for him, even fiercer than his was for her, and the passion she had spent upon his body. And how eventually he had responded in kind, at first almost overwhelmed but soon an eager and equal partner in their lovemaking, drawn in by her salacity and quickly apace with it. Even the memory was seductive.

But the fire! The thought snapped into his mind as if to

189

scold him. Yet the fire was no more than the phantom flames of his imagination. *That couldn't be, that really couldn't be!* He hadn't imagined the heat, the awful clogging smoke fumes. God, what had happened to him in that cellar? *Leave now,* the voice urged. *Let them wallow in their own wretchedness.*

Ash shoved himself away from the wall and walked doggedly towards the door that would take him out into the sharp freshness of the night. It opened as he was grasping the handle, a young couple coming through, the youth's arm around the girl's waist. Ash stood aside and the youth nodded, barely glancing at him. They disappeared into the saloon bar, the girl tittering at something her escort was whispering to her.

Ash stepped out into the high street, pulling the lapels of his coat up around his neck once more as the chill bit. The inn door slowly swung shut and with it went the warmth of its light.

He stiffened when he saw the old Wolseley parked at the kerbside. Christina's shadowed face watched him through the windscreen.

He lingered, undecided. Then he strolled over and opened the passenger door, the vehicle's metal hinges groaning as he did so. Leaning forward, he peered in.

'Why did you leave?' There was anger in Christina's question.

Ash was taken aback. 'Why did I –? Oh Christ, I don't believe it.'

'You didn't tell anyone where you were going.'

His anger was equal to hers as he got into the car. 'There was no one to tell! What happened, Christina? Why was the house empty?'

She reached forward and switched on the engine.

'I asked you a question,' Ash said evenly.

'I let you sleep. You were exhausted, I could see that.'

'I asked you where you were,' he persisted.

She engaged gear and the Wolseley pulled away from the kerb.

'Hey, wait a minute – where d'you think you're going?'

'Back to Edbrook, of course,' she replied, eyes on the road.

'I'm not sure –'

She looked quickly at him. 'You're not running out, are you? After last night?'

His temples throbbed and he squeezed them with his fingertips. 'What happened between us . . .'

'Was good. Don't you remember how good it was?'

'It's difficult to . . . I'm confused, Christina. I'm bloody weary and I'm confused.'

The car sped through the village, swiftly reaching the outskirts, the darkness taking on substance beneath the trees where moonlight could not reach.

Ash angled himself in his seat so that he could look at her. 'What's happening at Edbrook, Christina? I don't understand what's going on. Are you and your brothers playing some lunatic trick?'

She was silent, concentrating on driving, the car's speed steadily increasing. He could smell the oldness of the Wolseley now, and a metallic dampness that suggested rust lurked between joinings and wheel arches.

'There is no ghost, is there?' he went on. 'It's something you all dreamed up. For some sick reason you wanted to get at me. Tell my why. Please tell me.'

The car rounded a curve in the road, tyres protesting against the pressure as speed was maintained.

'For God's sake answer me. Tell me what you're up to, Christina.'

Her foot pressed the accelerator pedal down further.

'You never had a twin sister, did you? It was all a lie, part of the act.'

'You wanted to leave before completing the investigation,' Christina said.

'Aren't you listening to me? Haven't you heard a word I've said? You never had a twin who died when you were kids. There was no such sister. I believe one thing though: there *is* a schizophrenic among the Mariells.' He gripped the back of his seat as the car lurched round another bend. 'It's you, isn't it, Christina?'

She was taut, staring straight ahead, her profile, save for her brow which remained in shadow, pure and unblemished in the moonlight that shone through the windscreen.

Frustrated by her lack of response, Ash reached in his pocket for his cigarettes and lighter. He managed a grin, but it was sardonic.

'I should have realized. All that talk about the Mariells, how private their family affairs were through each generation. Madness isn't something you acknowledge, is it, let alone discuss?'

He flicked out the lighter and noticed Christina flinch from the flame. The nervousness in her sideways glance gave him a childish satisfaction. Let the flame burn.

'Have Robert and Simon always protected you, Christina? Nanny Tess, too?'

He moved the lighter closer to her face, perhaps to see her more clearly, perhaps to torment her. The car slowed and turned into a smaller lane, passing the telephone box Ash had tried to use earlier that day.

Christina cringed away from him now, but still she faced the front, continuing to drive, the Wolseley picking up speed once more. Occasionally, as if the tiny fire had some irresistible influence, her eyes would dart towards it. Just as fast they would return to the road ahead.

Ash, although conscious of his malice, enjoyed her discomfort. Blame it on the booze, he reassured himself as he taunted Christina with the lighter. Regard it as a small repayment for the nightmare she and her family had given him.

'I don't know how you did it, Christina, how you and your brothers created those effects – the fire in the cellar, the . . .' he flicked his other hand in the air in a hopeless gesture '. . . the girl I . . . I thought was in the pond. But then, you're all very clever, aren't you, all pretty smart? But not quite right . . .'

He thrust the flame closer to her cheek.

Christina recoiled, turning her face aside, and the car swerved dangerously. He grabbed her wrist with his free hand to steady the wheel, afraid they would crash.

There was something peculiar about the flesh he held.

He looked down at her hand and the unlit cigarette fell from his lips, for the fingers that curled around the steering wheel were no more than blackened bone, streaky mounds that might have been crisped meat clinging to them. The gristle beneath his grip seemed to flake as his hold involuntarily tightened.

Christina's head slowly came away from the side window it had rested against. He saw her smile in profile before she had completed the turn towards him. Moonlight illuminated the other side of her face.

He screamed.

For her skin was charred and withered, the fleshy lids that should have been around her eye rotted away so that the eyeball was incredibly large and staring. Her scalp was bare and glistening on that side, long single strands of hair hanging in wisps. The lips at the corner of her mouth had been burned away, exposing her teeth and dark gums, so that her smile had degenerated to a grotesque grin.

Ash dropped the lighter in shock, the flame immediately snuffed. But in the moonlight, the huge eyeball continued to stare at him from the silvery reflection of what was once her face.

TWENTY-SEVEN

The Wolseley careered erratically, yet did not decrease its speed along the narrow lane. Thin branches of hedges flayed the side windows as the car's tyres chewed grooves in the grassy shoulders. Still Christina – or the thing she now was – kept her foot firm on the accelerator.

Ash had shrunk away from her, his back rigid against the passenger door. She was once again in profile and he could see the sweetness of her half-smile. But his mind could see the mutilation hidden from view on the other side.

The stone pillars of Edbrook's gates loomed up and the car rushed through them, scarcely losing speed in the turn. Ash was thrown forward, his head crashing against glass; he hardly felt the blow. The dark shape of the house at the end of the drive grew rapidly in the windscreen.

He opened his mouth – whether to scream or to protest was of no consequence, for no sound came from his constricted throat – as they roared past the gardens on either side of the drive.

The Wolseley screeched to a side-sliding halt outside Edbrook, spraying gravel against the stonework, and Ash almost tumbled to the floor.

He twisted round to fumble for the door handle, refusing

to look at the dreadful thing beside him inside the old vehicle, desperate to be away from such close and enclosed proximity to it. He drew in a sharp breath that might easily have been a sob when he found the handle.

Almost falling through the open door, Ash launched himself into a staggering run, in his panic failing to notice the other vehicle nestled beneath the low branches of a tree on the far side of the forecourt. He thought he heard a dry rasping laughter, the kind that might be forced from a scorched throat, coming from the Wolseley behind him.

He climbed the three stone steps, tripping on the last one so that he collapsed heavily against the double-door of the house. Using one of the brass doorknobs for support, he hauled himself up, thumping against the wood with the flat of his fist as he did so.

On his feet once more, he looked over his shoulder towards the parked vehicle. The driver's door was opening. He could hear a scratchy kind of chuckling.

Ash flailed at the front door with both fists, ignoring the juddering shocks that ran through both arms, trying to call out but the terrible tightness in his throat muscles preventing him from doing so.

Although he dared not look directly again, his head half-turned as if irresistibly drawn, so that he perceived movement in the periphery of his vision. Christina was emerging from the car.

His chest heaved with what could be nothing other than a terrified wail; his blows against the door became slower, less hopeful. He wanted to run from there, to escape before the approaching figure reached him. Yet he suddenly felt so languid, so weary, a dread-filled heaviness sinking through his limbs, dragging at his strength. He knew, without looking, that she had reached the first step. His scream was stifled within his breast. He heard the scraping of a shoe against stone.

He almost lost his balance as the door before him yawned inwards.

There was nothing welcoming in Nanny Tess' demeanour; she grimaced, began to say something. But he had already pushed past her before any words could form, and had slammed the door behind him so that the aunt could only stand back in surprise, whatever she had meant to say already forgotten.

Trembling so violently that his fingers scrabbled against the lock, Ash turned the key, the metallic *clunk* satisfying but not reassuring enough. He crouched to shoot the bolt into its floor socket, repeating the process on the neighbouring side. He rose and leaned his back against the barrier as if to add weight.

Ash could not help the low moan that escaped him when he saw the changed condition of Edbrook.

The lights were even dimmer than before, like grey candle-glows, as though they, too, were part of the degenerative process; but they were strong enough to reveal the grime on the ceilings and walls, the dust-filled cobwebs, the mould that spread from corners and recesses, the long, dark cracks in the wood panelling. Strips of tattered wallpaper hung loose above the oak panels, and scraps that might have been fallen plaster from the ceiling littered the hall floor. And all-pervading was the pungency of decay, the redolent perfume of empti-ness.

Robert and Simon Mariell watched him from the stairs.

His speechlessness at last broke. 'For God's sake – *Christina!*'

The two brothers smiled.

There came a quiet tapping from behind him.

Ash spun around as if he had been touched; he stepped away from the threshold.

The tapping stopped.

He cried out when the double-door was shaken in its frame by thunderous, powerful blows. The barrier strained against its hinges, the wood seeming to bow inwards, as though something were pressing from the other side; small jagged cracks appeared on the surface, joining to form a hairline pattern.

Ash slowly backed away, his eyes riveted to the bulging wood, its creaking groans abnormally loud.

Abruptly the pressure from without ceased. There was total silence.

Until Robert said from the stairway: 'Please open the door, Nanny.'

To Ash's horror, the Mariells' aunt went forward and turned the key in the lock.

'No, don't let her in!' he implored.

Nanny Tess hesitated. She looked at Ash uncertainly, then at her nephew. Robert, still smiling benignly, gave a single nod of his head. Nanny Tess reached down to release the bolt.

With a movement that was surprising in its swiftness, she flung open one side of the double-door. A shadowy figure stood outside.

Ash felt something drain from him, a palpable loss, as if any warmth in his veins and tissue had been syphoned away, leaving his body leaden and cold. When he fled, it was awkwardly, his feet barely lifting from the floor. The stairs were mountainous, his attempt to climb them ponderous.

Robert continued to smile as Ash pushed by him. Simon, hands tucked nonchalantly into trouser pockets, sniggered.

Ash used the rail to draw himself upwards. Now that he had consciously forced himself into flight, his fear in some self-preserving way began to overwhelm the stupefying dread so that strength, enfeebled though it was, gradually returned and his efforts gained momentum. He stumbled near the top, but kept going, using hands and knees to drag himself forward, scrabbling over the last step, rising to stagger down the darkened corridor towards the bedroom they had given him.

The door was open and once inside he slammed it shut, quickly locking it. He leaned his soaked forehead against the painted wood and tried to control his rapid breathing so that he could listen for noises outside. He was certain he could hear approaching footsteps.

His eyes closed for a moment as if in supplication.

He shoved himself away from the door and tugged at the hefty chest of drawers nearby, sliding it over, using sideways to and fro movements to make the journey easier, jamming the chest against the door as a barricade, creating a defence that he hoped would be impossible for anyone outside to get through. He slapped down the light switch and the bulb in the centre of the room flickered and wavered beneath its shade before settling to a dim glow.

He trod backwards from the door, his gaze never leaving it, retreating to the other side of the room, as far away from the barricade as possible.

Soon there was the familiar tapping from outside.

His name was whispered.

'Leave me alone!' he shouted, hysteria close enough to raise the pitch of his voice. *'Just leave me alone!'*

His cry became plaintive, almost a moan, as he sank miserably into the armchair opposite the door.

'Just leave me alone . . .'

The whispering stopped.

TWENTY-EIGHT

Nothing stirred in the house called Edbrook.

No footsteps along the dingy corridors and hallways; no movement inside dusty rooms save for the scratchy scurryings of vermin who nestled in the sagging underbellies of sofas, or the sluggish tottering of spiders drugged by the late season's climate; no inner breeze nudged curtains or drapes. The stone walls held their peace. The dawn hung colourlessly against windows.

In an upstairs room a man slept fretfully in an armchair facing a barricaded door.

David Ash still wore his rumpled overcoat, its collar turned up around his neck. His bearded chin sagged against his chest. His face was sallow in the dim light, features heavy with fatigue, his brow troubled by the images of his sleep in which . . .

. . . the boy wakes and listens to the whispered call.
'David . . .'

He leaves the bedroom, drawn by the gentle voice and descends the stairs to the candlelit place below. A coffin stands at the far end of the long room.

The boy approaches, his eyes enlarged and fear-stricken. He peers down into the silk-lined casket.

The girl who lies there is not his sister.

She is older, and she is beautiful in death.

Her eyes open.

She smiles.

The smile corrupts to a grin.

Christina reaches as if to embrace him.

She whispers:

'David . . .'

Ash awoke with a choked cry, the startled jerk of his body upsetting the empty vodka bottle by his foot. He looked around as if mystified by his surroundings. Vapid light from the window integrated drearily with the ceiling light so that there was an oddness to the room, a lack of depth to its shadings, a neutrality to its brighter tones. He blinked to ease the soreness of his eyes, knowing without seeing that they were red-rimmed; he felt the puffiness of their lids. Ash swallowed, throat dry, running his fingers through the tangle of his hair as he did so.

His hand stopped when he recalled the dream; and he moaned faintly when he saw the heavy chest of drawers rammed against the bedroom door, remembering why it was there.

Ash held his breath, forcing himself to listen, his hands quivering slightly on the arms of the chair. There was only silence from outside and somehow he sensed that peculiar vacuity extended beyond the corridor: the whole house was quiet as if, like him, it was holding its breath.

He lurched from the seat and went to the barricade, leaning on the chest for support, listening further, waiting for any shift in atmosphere, the slightest bump or scuffle from outside. There was nothing.

He walked unsteadily back to the window, his coordination slow in returning, senses not yet fully alert, and looked out at the gardens below. A fine drizzle of rain was sending up a thin mist from the ground so that the statues out there were vague, ill-defined forms.

Resolution came to Ash as the dulling effects of his troubled sleep gradually dispersed.

Taking the holdall from the wardrobe, he began throwing clothing and other personal items into it, not bothering with neatness, bundling them in haphazardly, pushing everything tight to make room, his efforts gaining momentum, becoming a rush. He threw in his notes and diagrams from the small bureau he'd used as a desk, then zipped up the bag, muttering when loose clothing snagged the catch, but unwilling to spend time disengaging it. He stood on tip-toe to reach the suitcase on top of the wardrobe and laid it open on the bed. He studied its emptiness for a few moments, knowing he would have to retrieve the equipment from various parts of the house.

Ash looked over at the door again.

Cautiously he went to the chest of drawers and gripped its edges. Summoning up his strength, he heaved it aside. One hand still on top of the chest to steady himself, Ash nervously regarded the key in the lock of the door. He had to force himself to turn it. And then had to force himself to open the door.

Nanny Tess was standing outside.

'Jesus –' he said almost as a breath.

She stepped into the light, her face distraught, seeming more aged, her features more deeply lined. There was a pallid greyness to her skin, the lack of colour that sometimes comes with long illness.

Her voice was urgent, but kept low, as if she were afraid that others might hear. 'You must leave immediately. You must go right away, Mr Ash.'

'Where are they?' he asked her, his own voice hushed.

'Never mind that.' It was almost a reprimand. 'Don't ask any questions of me, just leave this house now. It's no longer a game – it's become more than that. Something has happened that's changed everything. They're angry with you, Mr Ash. Terribly angry.'

She leaned back to glance out the door, as though to make sure the corridor was still empty. She bent towards him again, her manner conspiratorial. 'There's an early morning train that stops at the village station to deliver mail. You've got time to catch it if you hurry.'

Ash needed no further bidding. He returned to the bed to collect the holdall and his eyes briefly lingered on the open suitcase. He turned away, leaving it lying there; somehow the equipment, the very tools of his trade, no longer seemed important.

Gripping the holdall, he made for the door and stopped in surprise when he discovered the old lady had gone. He went out into the corridor. And became very still.

The dog was watching him from the far end, a bunched, threatening shape.

Ash slowly moved away, treading warily, afraid that any hasty action, any hint of panic, would set the animal on him. Its growl rumbled down the corridor and Ash willed himself to back off smoothly, to do nothing that would excite the dog.

Seeker began to stalk him.

Ash's grip on the holdall tightened. If the brute charged he would push the bag into those powerful jaws, use it as a shield. What then? How long could he hold the dog off? If he returned to the bedroom he would be trapped. Perhaps he should call out, bring Nanny Tess back to him. She might be able to control Seeker. But then why hadn't she waited? Was that part of the plan, to lure him from the bedroom and leave him at the mercy of this beast? Christ, were they all crazy in this house?

Seeker kept a measured distance, pacing its prey with matching steps. Two dull pinpoints of light were all that Ash could see of its eyes in the dimness of the corridor; its massive head was tucked close into muscled shoulders so that it seemed a shapeless mass was gliding forward.

Without taking his attention from the trailing beast, Ash knew he was nearing the gallery overlooking the hallway. *Had* he looked he would have caught sight of the figure rising up from the stairway. Only when he heard a peculiarly wheezed chuckle did he glance over his shoulder.

Simon was at the top of the stairs. Although it wasn't *quite* Simon.

Even in the poor light Ash could discern the deathly paleness of Christina's brother, almost as though his face and hands had been dusted with fine white powder. And his skin was withered, puckered and blemished in parts as though rotting. Beneath the collar of his open shirt, his neck was discoloured with purple bruising, vivid against his unnatural pallor, and the flesh there was deeply indented, his head tilted awkwardly to one side.

Despite his unsightly appearance, Simon was smiling pleasantly.

For no other reason than utter shock, Ash hurled the bag at the figure at the top of the stairway, the sudden movement provoking the dog behind him into launching itself forward.

Ash heard the scuffling of its paws, the altered pitch of its snarling, and did not waste time in turning towards the charge. He slid over the balustrade, grabbing the rail as his body began to fall. He clung there, feet kicking space, until Seeker's jaws appeared above him, its teeth snapping air. Ash's hold loosened and he plunged, clutching momentarily at the lip of the balcony, but unable to sustain the grip. He fell to the floor, landing heavily and gasping at the jarring pain in his ankle.

He lay there on his back, struggling for breath, his whole body numbed by the fall. As the numbness matured to an aching tenderness, he became conscious of the wisps of smoke curling in the air. He listened to the distant crackle of fire and felt – although it might have been imagined – heat against his face.

Now he heard padding footsteps on the stairs.

Ash rolled to a kneeling position, pushing himself upright, the pain in his ankle severe. He glimpsed Seeker as it rounded the post at the foot of the stairs, skidding on the unswept floor, but quickly regaining its balance and bounding forwards.

Ash hobbled away, knowing his only chance was to put a barrier between himself and the rushing animal. The kitchen was too far along the hall – he would make it. He pushed open the nearest door. The cellar door.

A wall of blinding flame sent him staggering backwards, his arms raised to protect his face.

But he had already caught sight of something moving in the fire below. A figure had been climbing the cellar steps, rising slowly as if oblivious of the heat. Ash parted his arms so that he could look again, bewildered, not believing what he had seen.

The figure had nearly reached the top step and it was ablaze, a person totally engulfed in bleached, billowing flame. And yet its countenance, the reddened, boiling mess that was its face, was familiar.

The human torch that emerged from the cellar was Robert Mariell.

T W E N T Y - N I N E

Seeker stopped, twin fiery images dancing in its liquid eyes as though the man burned inside the dog's own skull. It cowered and began to shiver; from its slathering jaws there now came piteous whining.

Ash waited no longer. He limped from the furnace that was the cellar, away from the flaming, blistering figure and its stench of roasting.

The dog shook itself, aware that its quarry was escaping. It warily skirted the enflamed man, head hung low until it was past, then gave chase once more.

Ash paused only to throw a hall chair at his pursuer. The missile bounced in front of Seeker, momentarily interrupting the dog's flight. Simon Mariell was now at the foot of the stairs, his grotesqueness lit by the incineration of his elder brother, his derisory laughter hissing through a strangulated throat.

Ash dodged into the kitchen, twisting to swing the door shut behind him. It was almost closed when Seeker's jaws appeared and its teeth locked onto the sleeve of his coat.

He tried to pull his arm free, keeping pressure on the door, pushing it hard against the animal's muzzle. Ash yelled when he finally tore his arm away, the dog toppling backwards into the hall with scraps of material in its mouth. Ash slammed the door shut and stood back as Seeker launched itself at the other side, the timber screeching in its frame, but mercifully holding. There followed a frantic scratching against the wood.

Through the squalid and littered kitchen hurried Ash, his injured ankle jarring at every step. He reached the back door and wrenched it open.

Cold morning air rushed at him as if welcoming him to freedom. Ash limped outside, glorying in the light rain on his face, sucking in pure air, cleansing his lungs of Edbrook's malodour. He had broken out and the liberation pumped energy into his system. He wanted to scream with the pure relief.

It was not until he was at the edge of the terrace that he dared look back at the house. In the rain its stone was even darker, windows even blacker. Still, it was just a house, bricks, timber and glass, a manmade place and nothing more than that. An old building that appeared weary with its own age, made sinister to him only because *he* knew of the aberration within its walls. He wiped raindrops from his eyes. It was all impossible, all unreal; yet he was not dreaming.

But the very real nightmare continued when the glass of a lower window shattered outwards and the demon-shape of Seeker hurtled through.

Ash hobbled down the steps from the terrace into the gardens and loped along the flagstone path, realizing he would never outdistance the pursuing dog. He looked back over his shoulder and saw that Seeker had reached the top of the steps. The dog began an unhurried descent, as if aware its prey could not escape. Its mouth was wet with white-flecked spittle, its coat shiny with rain; it slunk along the path, head hunched into shoulders that quivered with pent-up force, jaws opening in a deep snarling.

Ash confronted the stalking beast, backing away as he had before, having no choice but to play the cruel cat and mouse game, for he was too afraid to run. The beast would maul him badly, there was no doubting that; the question was whether it was savage – or powerful – enough to kill him. The rain failed to cool the clammy heat of Ash's body.

Seeker was only yards away, the distance between them quickly narrowing. Ash half-crouched, continuing to move backwards, frightened but angry, too, that he should be so intimidated by a dog. An obscenity formed on his lips, a useless but defiant oath to hurl at the creature. Before he could scream it though, his heel touched something solid. He could move no further: the low wall of the stagnant pond was behind him. Seeker tensed its muscles, ready to attack.

The water behind Ash erupted.

He stumbled round, the animal forgotten. Rising over him was a vision so terrifying that he collapsed to his knees.

What was left of her hair trailed to her shoulders in sodden, tousled strands. The long, bedraggled gown she wore was stained with slime from the pond, much of the material hanging in scorched tatters around her, slithering green vegetation clinging to her body as though it had attached itself while she lay dormant beneath the water's surface.

Seeker howled and sank its belly against the path.

She clutched the edge of the wall with scummy, shrunken hands, one of them only blackened gristle, her rictus grin fixed on Ash. Almost half her body was burned raw, much of it charred brittle. As it had the night before, one huge, exposed eye stared unblinkingly at him.

She dragged herself from the pond, water draining from her to create a puddle around her scarred feet. He had fallen away as she emerged, and now she loomed over and reached out her arms towards him, slick, thin weeds draped like bracelets from her wrists.

Ash shuffled his body away in abhorrence and what was left of her rotted lips curled back: the scratchy intonation that came from them might have been his name.

She screeched as her darkened side abruptly burst into flame.

A whiteness, a total banishment of thought, caused by the shock wiped his mind. Sheer reaction drove him to his feet.

Ash ran from the writhing figure, the agonized shrieks accompanying him as though inside his head, just behind that screen of whiteness. And as he drew away, the blankness started to disintegrate, her cries becoming louder as they pushed through the fading barrier; yet there was also laughter, a distant mocking sound, no more than an echo.

He slipped on the damp grass, pain shooting up from his ankle to his groin. He picked himself up, the searing spasm of little consequence, and stumbled across neglected flower beds, through bushes, making for the trees, seeking shelter, the screams and the laughter now gone from his head, left behind in the gardens to diminish, though never quite to fade.

The rain began to fall more heavily, making his journey treacherous. His hands were held before him to brush away leafy branches as he entered the woodland. They guided him around trees, his vision blurred by the rain and perhaps his own tears. He was sure there were others in the woods with him, for he could hear snickering, their soft derisive calls; occasionally he caught sight of their flitting forms as they kept pace with him, though at a distance, among the trees.

He had no idea where he was running to except that it was away from the estate. Once he reached a road he would make his way to the village somehow, back to the world of order, to sweet, mundane normality. A rustling of bushes sent him veering off to the left. An unclear shape in the shadows beneath a tree caused him to run to his right. Mocking laughter from behind increased his laboured pace.

Soon he came to a clearing, one with which he was familiar. He stumbled, dropping to his hands and knees so that the rain, unimpeded by the canopy of trees, beat against his back. Ash realized where he was, for before him, so solid that it appeared to have risen up from the earth itself, was the stone monument of the Mariells' family tomb.

He gasped in deep lungfuls of drenched air, his shoulders heaving, his hair matted against his skull. Rain pounded against the grey slabs of the mausoleum, its force causing a shimmering halo. The stone was slowly being cleansed of its mud and grime, lichen between cracks taking on a deeper hue, grass at its base bent under the pressure. As he watched, dirt was washed from the deeply etched inscription by the side of the entrance.

He could not help but read the names as they were slowly unveiled:

THOMAS EDWARD MARIELL
1896 – 1938

◆◆◆

ISOBEL ELOISE MARIELL
1902 – 1938

Ash blinked rain from his eyes as sediment ingrained in the lettering began to flow more freely, joining with the surrounding dirt in a falling wash of sludge. His lips moved like an infant's as he silently read the rest of the chiselled inscription, and fresh horror compounded that which already rooted him there.

BELOVED CHILDREN
◆◆◆

ROBERT
1919 – 1949

SIMON
1923 – 1949

CHRISTINA
1929 – 1949

The last date, the year of death, became enlarged in his mind, as though it had grown in the stone.

1949

From the tomb's dingy interior came the hollow giggle of a young child.

He saw that the iron gate was open wide. He heard a different sound from within, the grating of stone against stone. There was a stirring amidst the mausoleum's twilight interior, a flat slab that was a coffin lid shifting sideways. On another tier, a stone lid was rising as if pushed from beneath.

The child giggled again.

THIRTY

He thrashed through the undergrowth, falling, rising, never stopping, cruel branches whipping at his face and hands, snagging his clothes, concealed obstacles tripping him when they could, birds screeching their own frenzied haranguing. Ash kept running, never once looking back, afraid of what might be following him through the woodland. He pushed by leafy barriers, scrambled over fallen tree trunks, always onwards, fighting through the tangled areas until at last, at long last, he saw a break in the landscape ahead.

With an explosive shout of relief, Ash staggered out onto the road.

He allowed himself a few brief moments to recover his breath, listening for pursuers while he did so. All now seemed quiet back there. Whoever – *whatever*, for he had not stayed to find out – had been inside the mausoleum had not followed him. Nevertheless, he set off again at an awkward jog, his injured left leg dragging, his throat raw from the harshness of his breathing. The morning had lightened, the rain having lost its ferocity, now only a drizzle.

He was not aware of the vehicle approaching from behind until it was a hundred yards or so away. He heard the engine, the tyres softly crushing twigs fallen from overhanging branches, and looked back to see headlights shining palely through the rain. He tried desperately to run faster, but the extra strength just wasn't there: his strides became more clumsy, more lumbering.

The headlights brightened the wet road. Ash kept going, despair dragging at him, his steps becoming wilder as he strayed erratically over the road.

The Wolseley drew alongside and he stumbled away to avoid its wheels. The driver's window was open, a hand reached out. Nanny Tess called to him. 'Mr Ash. Please get in. You're exhausted, you'll never make it on your own.'

He came to a tottering halt, bent almost double, retching air. Hysteria was close when he finally managed to say, 'What . . . what d'you want from me?'

Her face was concerned, her eyes pitying. 'I only want to help you,' she told him. 'Please get in, let me take you to the station. It's your only chance.'

Ash knew she was right: he was too weary both physically and mentally to get there by his own efforts. He slumped across the bonnet of the car.

'Just tell me why,' he pleaded. 'Why did they do it to me?'

She indicated the passenger door. 'Get in, Mr Ash, before you collapse in the road.'

Using the bonnet for support, he limped around the other side of the car, realizing he had no other choice but to trust her. He fell leadenly into the passenger seat.

The car moved forward again, picking up speed gradually. Ash, his chest still heaving, limbs trembling, regarded her with suspicion. Nanny Tess had altered considerably, but not in the unnatural way of her nephews and niece. She was haggard, her hair unkempt. The lines of her face were not only etched deeper, but there were more of them, patterning her whitish skin, hardly any part of her face free of their graining.

'They were wrong to do this to you,' she said in a querulous voice. 'I warned them not to, I begged them.'

Unsteadily, in a sigh, he said, 'I don't understand any of it.'

She snatched a look at him, frowning at his condition. 'Oh, you weren't meant to. They wanted to confuse you. That would make you more frightened.'

'Why should they want to frighten me?' he snapped. 'What have I ever done to them?'

Wipers smoothed the last patchy raindrops from the windscreen.

'They wanted to prove you wrong. All your theories, your disbelief in life after death – they wanted to make you see . . . to make you pay . . .'

He stared at her uncomprehendingly.

'There was no twin, Mr Ash,' she said quietly.

He made a noise of disgust. 'I realized that. Christina's the schizophrenic, isn't she?'

'Is? You still don't understand? After all that's happened?' She looked at him again and Ash avoided her gaze. 'It was as though there were two souls inhabiting her body, one normal, a sweet, loving spirit – the other a mad thing, a spiteful, malicious being. We kept that part of her hidden, away from the eyes of outsiders.'

Her brown-spotted hands tightened on the steering wheel. 'After Isobel and Thomas died, it was left to the two boys and myself to protect Christina, to control her as best we could. But oh, it was heart-breaking when we had to lock her away for her own safety as well as ours.'

She slowed the car as they approached a junction. Ash was almost tempted to run over to the telephone box on the grass verge. But what would be the point? It was easier to get to the station and then as far away from this damnable place as possible. Nanny Tess turned into the wider road, the car gathering speed once more. The windscreen wipers scraped noisily over the glass that had become dry. She did not seem to notice.

The aunt spoke in sadness, as though memories were hardly dimmed by time. Weary, beaten, Ash listened.

'Simon was the cause of the final tragedy. You see, their childish ways followed them into adulthood, even though the boys had been warned to treat Christina with care. Perhaps Simon grew tired of her split personality – she was so full of fun one moment, a biting, screaming wretch the next – or perhaps one day he just became frightened of her.'

She paused, suddenly aware of the wipers' dry screeching. To Ash's relief, she switched them off.

'Robert was on his way back from London after a meeting with his financial advisers and I'd gone to collect him from the station. I . . . I thought Simon was able enough to cope. Perhaps it was another game, just another one of his foolish pranks.' She fell silent.

'Tell me . . .' he urged quietly.

She seemed to gather her resolve. 'Simon locked Christina in the wine cellar with her pet. He knew she hated it down there, hated the darkness, the smell of damp, those solid, windowless walls around her. Somehow she managed to light a fire. I often had to search her for matches; she was fascinated by those tiny flames. Christina used to tell me that when a flame died, the smoke that curled into the air was its tiny soul on the way to Heaven.'

Nanny Tess smiled bitterly as she remembered. Her expression soon stiffened to grimness.

'She may have been playing when she lit the fire in the cellar, or it may have been deliberate – there's no way of knowing. Perhaps she only wanted to frighten Simon into releasing her. But it got out of hand: the fire spread.

'Robert and I returned from the village to find the cellar filled with flames. Simon was crouched opposite the open door, weeping, just pointing at the fire and weeping. We could hear Christina's screams from below, we could hear Seeker's terrible howling.

'Robert rushed down there, despite the heat, the flames . . .'

The car's wheels crackled over a tree branch lying in the road, the gunfire sound startling Ash.

Nanny Tess was oblivious. 'Minutes later, two figures emerged from that furnace. The first was Christina. Her clothes were on fire, one side of her body was burning.'

The old woman closed her eyes at the thought, and Ash anxiously looked at the road ahead, then back at her. She was watching the road again, driving steadily.

'She was too quick for us. She ran by and we were distracted by the other . . . the other figure. Robert was completely ablaze. I . . . I don't know how he climbed the stairs . . . he collapsed at our feet . . . in such agony, oh, he was in such agony . . .

'We tried to save him, tried to beat out the flames. But it was no use – his whole body was a ball of fire. His screams . . . I still hear his screams ringing through the house at night. Even when I've taken pills to make me sleep, I still hear those terrible, agonized screams.'

'You found Christina –' Ash began to say.

'Yes, Mr Ash. She'd thrown herself into the pond and she drowned there. As I told you before, she must have been too hurt, too weakened, to drag herself out again.'

Ash rested his head back, one elbow against the sill of the passenger window, his hand covering his eyes. 'Oh Jesus . . .' he breathed.

'In those days we had grounds staff and they rushed into the house and managed to contain the blaze until the fire services arrived. Otherwise, I suppose Edbrook would have burned to the ground. That might have been a blessing.'

Again that haunted, faraway smile. It quickly dissolved.

'Simon was distraught, inconsolable. He blamed himself for the deaths of his brother and sister. You see, despite their teasing, they had been very close, especially so after their mother and father were killed. Simon hanged himself from the stairway a few weeks later.'

Ash, in spite of all he had been through looked incredulously at the old woman. He wondered if she were insane. 'It's not possible,' he said. 'None of this is possible. I saw them all, I spoke to them. For Christ's sake, I *ate* with them, Christina drove me in the car!'

Nanny Tess was shaking her head.

'Christina . . .' Ash insisted '. . . I touched her! We . . . she was warm living flesh!' But he remembered the iciness of the bed where she had lain.

'You saw and talked with no living thing. We were alone in the house, Mr Ash, just you and I. But not really alone. Robert, Simon and Christina were with us, but not as living people. Seeker too – its poor innocent soul is so confused.'

'You're crazy,' Ash said tonelessly.

There was something more than sorrow behind her smile this time. 'Did you feel weakened inside the house, Mr Ash? With all your knowledge of parapsychology, didn't you realize that your own psychic energy was being used, being drained from you, just as they've drained mine through all these years? That's how they exist, don't you see?

'They return to Edbrook time and time again, existing off me – *dear Nanny Tess, the caretaker of Edbrook, the children's guardian in life and in death* – continuing to play their games as though somehow that held their spirits together, bound them close to each other. I think they consider the game they've played with you to be their finest. I only hope – I pray – it's to be their last.'

There was no conviction when he said, 'They were real . . .'

'Only in your mind. And the human mind is a mysterious place, perhaps as strange as this other world where their souls truly exist. They used your mind, they sought its deepest levels and used the thoughts hiding there.'

He shook his head disbelievingly.

'Do you have that tiny tape recorder with you?' she asked.

Numbly, his thoughts elsewhere, Ash delved beneath his overcoat to search his jacket pockets. He brought out the micro-recorder.

'Switch it on, Mr Ash,' she told him, and he was puzzled by the note of smugness in the instruction. 'Play back the recording you made at Edbrook.'

Without dissent, he pressed the REWIND button, waiting for the left spool to reclaim tape. There was a quiet hissing when he pressed PLAY, then Ash's metallically thin voice came from the machine.

'*How did your parents die, Christina?*'

The quiet hissing of running tape and atmospherics followed.

'*You were just kids when it happened?*' came his voice again. No reply.

Frowning, he rewound further, then pressed PLAY again.

'*– anyone you know? Have known?*' he heard himself say. He remembered this was part of a question he had put to Simon.

Silence save for the tape's own sound.

Now dismayed, he pressed REWIND.

'*. . . even been known to affect electricity.*' His words.

No response.

His own voice once more: '*No, I'm still talking about unexplained phenomena. Please go on with what you were telling me.*'

He listened to the hissing for only a short while before angrily switching off the machine. He noticed that the first houses of the village were in view as he shoved the recorder back into his pocket.

With a curious mixture of detachment and perplexity he asked: 'Why? Why me?'

Her sigh was as weary as his question and Ash realized that Nanny Tess scarcely resembled the person he had first met at Edbrook, the reserved spinster, the proper maiden aunt.

'An alliance,' she said in answer.

He shook his head, not understanding.

'An alliance of spirits,' she went on, driving carefully through the deserted high street. 'A joint game between them and another, someone they conspired with on the other side. Someone close to you, Mr Ash.'

The muscles at the back of his neck tensed, a coldness swept through him. A new, deeper, dread was aroused within him. His desire had been to return to the world of normality, and he was now there, that condition just outside the car windows, with the houses and the shops they passed, the street signs, lampposts, the everyday order of natural things; but the *abnormal* had accompanied him, was with him inside the vehicle. Nanny Tess' voice was a drone, yet every word registered, part of him comprehending, part of him repudiating everything she said. And slowly, the dread began to over-whelm reason.

'Their game was enhanced by your own total rejection of the spirit's existence after death, a belief you've always hidden behind for your own protection. Isn't that true? Hasn't the guilt you felt over your own sister's death made you erect a wall of non-belief?' She continued, not waiting for a reply. 'Aren't you still, even after all these years, afraid that she'll come back and demand retribution, make you pay for what you did to her? I told you the mind was a mysterious place . . .'

The car drew up outside the small railway station and through the entrance Ash saw a train waiting at the platform. But he sat there in the car, senses in turmoil. He was trembling, small, jerky shakes of his head refuting what she had told him.

Nanny Tess had become agitated, too, her distress shown in eyes that glistened wetly. 'But it's gone too far. I tried to control it, tried desperately, but as always, I gave in to them. My guilt is as bad as yours – I promised Isobel I would take care of them and I let them all die. Every one of them. How can I be forgiven?'

She pressed her forehead against the steering wheel, hiding her face between her arms. Her misery stretched the words so that Ash could barely understand what she was saying. 'Now the worst has happened. Now there will be questions asked about Edbrook, about the Mariells.'

Through his shocked confusion, he managed to find some anger. 'That's the last thing I'd do, tell anyone what happened to me back there. Who the hell would believe me?'

'*You still don't understand, do you? The game has gone too far!* Someone else became involved, someone else whose heart isn't as strong as yours.'

She raised her brow from her arms, her features wizened with torment, her hair straggled around wrinkled cheeks. Nanny Tess turned leisurely, although her dread-filled eyes dispelled any illusion of dispassion; her head craned round so that she could peer over her shoulder towards the back seat.

Even though he desperately did not want to, he was compelled to follow her gaze.

Edith Phipps stared at him from the back seat. Yet her eyes were as dull as slate, her jaw locked open with its upper set of teeth resting on her lower lip, the dislodged dentures ridiculing her death. But there was no slackness to her features, no corpse's languor; if a corpse could have voice, then Edith would be screaming.

Ash recoiled against the dashboard. It was not horror that he felt, for there is a limit to even that extreme emotion; in those few frozen moments as he looked upon Edith's stiffened body, his sensibilities were scoured by the utmost despair so that he was left empty and almost impassive.

But when he heard the titter that came from Nanny Tess and saw the madness that cavorted behind her old, frightened eyes, reality jolted him into action.

Ash fled from the car.

THIRTY-ONE

He pushed by the startled porter who was just entering the shady ticket hall from the platform. Ash heard the man curse and shout after him, but refused to stop. The train was beginning to move out, slowly trundling forward as though its burden were too great.

Grabbing a carriage doorhandle, Ash limped alongside the train, matching its speed so that he could pull the door open and scramble in. He nearly lost his footing as he did so, but managed to clutch the edge of the doorframe and haul himself up. He collapsed in a heap across the compartment seat, but quickly pushed himself upright as the carriage door swung shut with the train's gathering momentum; his head lolled drunkenly against the high back of the seat. Ash listened to his own mumblings, the denial, the rejection, of all that had happened, his hands tugging at his open shirt collar as though breathing were difficult. Tepid sweat trickled into the hollow of his neck.

The train began to pick up a smoothness of rhythm, though its motion was still unhurried, and Ash thanked God that he was at last leaving this hell's-place behind, leaving Edbrook and the terrors it held for him, the Mariells whose existence depended entirely on the remorse and fears of the living, the housekeeper aunt whose guilt-ridden grief eventually had deranged her mind. Leaving them all, leaving Christina . . .

Confusion, impressions, sensations, jibed at him. Too much had happened during that brief time at Edbrook to be accepted, or even acknowledged. He had suffered absolute fear, yet he had also succumbed to an intense loving. And had made love. But to what? An apparition? That wasn't possible, surely that wasn't possible.

He shook his head, a desperate motion. For he knew the truth of it.

Robert and Simon and Christina were ghosts, and together they had intrigued with another who had once been close to him, a sister who had despised him even beyond her own life, who had conspired against him from the grave. And that conspiracy had brought her haunting to a perverse reality.

He became rigid. With his back to the engine, his view was of the long empty platform steadily sliding away from him. But now a figure came into view, the man's head turning with the passing of the train.

Robert Mariell smiled at Ash.

Soon another could be seen through the grimed compartment windows. Simon stood coatless, hands tucked into trouser pockets, his throat no longer scarred, his face no longer tilted. His grin was carefree as he watched Ash go by.

An empty stretch of concrete, then another person standing there, gazing up at the train with all the innocence of childhood. There was no ageing after death; she was still a little girl. Below the white dress, the one she had drowned in, she wore white ankle socks. Beside her, patient and unmoving, stood Seeker.

Ash lurched to the door window, wrenching it down with a guillotine's thud. He leaned out, stretching a hand towards her.

'Juliet!' he screamed.

He could see her face clearly now, could discern the pretty features that his own mind had always blurred before,

221

unwilling, to recognize – *determined not to* – and thus acknowledge her unnatural existence. Her lips were perfectly clear as they twisted to a smile; and the malignity of the smile was just as plain.

The vision receded with the progress of the train, the dog a black mark frozen next to her.

Ash's outcry was of aching sorrow. He called to her again, reaching towards the dwindling figure, tears streaking the dirt that smeared his face.

The hands that clawed at his shoulders from inside the compartment were vicious and strong. He clung to the window's frame, afraid he would be thrown out onto the rushing ground below. He fought back, managing to inch his body round so that he could face his assailant. Cruelly sharp fingernails raked his face.

Christina's eyes were closed almost to ugly slits. Her face was unmarked, her body untouched by fire, and yet this was still a different Christina from the one he had come to know. Before him raged the darker side of her earthly nature, the flawed creature whom the Mariell family had endeavoured to conceal from outsiders. Her hair was a wild mass around her face, her mouth sneered to a grimace. The glitterings in those blue-grey eyes were the highlights of her madness, her beauty hidden behind a harridan's mask.

She drove at him relentlessly, her gown of pure, flowing white tossed as though by the wind, scratching and spitting so furiously that he was forced into a corner. He held up his arms to protect his face, allowing her to beat him, too afraid to retaliate. But as the pain became intolerable, he began to react, began to flail out at her, shouting her name, frustration and rage overwhelming his fright.

And although he found himself striking at emptiness, he could not stop beating the air.

Moments passed before, exhausted, he allowed his arms to drop away. And further moments went by as his eyes warily searched the compartment for her. Eventually, he straightened, his body swaying with the roll of the carriage.

He felt the wetness trickling on his cheek and he raised a trembling hand to touch.

For a long time afterwards Ash stared at the blood on his fingertips.

E D B R O O K

Night has begun its claim as the wind sighs along the pitted drive towards the large neglected house. A motorcar from another era stands beneath the steps that lead into the house.

The building seems desolate, its interior cluttered with shadows.

But someone moves through its darkness, journeying from room to room, a woman of late years who hums a melancholy tune, a rhyme with which she once lullabied the children of this place; but that was long ago and the children are no more.

With her, the old woman carries a box of matches. She strikes each one and leaves it burning where she pleases.

The stone shell that is called Edbrook blackens with the fading light. But in a window there rises a flickering orange glow. Soon that warm glow is joined by another.

And then by another.